THE Alpha BET

THE Alpha BET

Stephanie Hale

flux™

Woodbury, Minnesota

First Edition
First Printing, 2010

Cover design by Ellen Dahl
Cover images © 2009 by Thomas Northcut/Lifesize/Getty Images;
    Image Source/PunchStock

Flux, an imprint of Llewellyn Publications

Library of Congress Cataloging-in-Publication Data
Hale, Stephanie.
  The Alpha bet / Stephanie Hale.—1st ed.
    p. cm.
  Summary: Grace Kelly Cook, a self-proclaimed "science geek," starts college by allowing her roommate to help with a makeover, kissing a cute boy, and pledging a sorority, but she fears what will happen when others learn that she lied about her family connections and is only sixteen.
  ISBN 978-0-7387-1574-2
  [1. Greek letter societies—Fiction. 2. Universities and colleges—Fiction 3. Dating (Social customs)—Fiction. 4. Self-actualization (Psychology)—Fiction.] I. Title.
  PZ7.H138244.Alp 2010
  [Fic]—dc22
                                          2009030639

Flux
Llewellyn Publications
A Division of Llewellyn Worldwide, Ltd.
2143 Wooddale Drive
Woodbury, MN 55125-2989, U.S.A.
www.fluxnow.com

Printed in the United States of America

ONE

"It's a dorm, Mom, not the Playboy Mansion," I whisper in her ear, hoping she'll stop throwing her evil eye looks around at all the kids in my new dorm.

"Tell that to the girl over there using doilies to cover her chest," she says, turning away disgustedly.

At the exact moment I turn to check out the doily girl, who is actually an adorable blonde wearing a crocheted bikini top and jean cutoffs, she raises her arm and tosses something in my direction. She covers her perfectly glossed lips with her hand in horror, and a second later, something smacks against my forehead and explodes. A water balloon. Mom screams like she's been shot while I stand dripping into the cardboard box full of clothes I'm carrying.

This is not exactly how I pictured my first day of college.

"Are you alright?" Mom asks, once she realizes it wasn't her that was hit.

"Physically, tiptop. Emotionally, not so much," I reply, dropping my box and using the end of my T-shirt to wipe the water off my glasses.

"Oh my gosh. I'm, like, so sorry," the blonde says, rushing up. She's wringing her hands like crazy and I know she really is sorry. "Marcus was right behind you and I was trying to get him," she explains.

"You need to get a better aim," Mom practically growls at her while scrutinizing her bikini top, for nipple showage no doubt.

"It's okay, really. I'm Grace Kelly," I say, holding my hand out to the blonde. She looks confused. It's a look I'm familiar with. You say Grace Kelly and most people automatically think of an elegant, poised beauty cut down in the prime of her life, not an unfashionable, four-eyed drowned rat.

"I'm Star," she says, coming to her senses. We shake hands and I try very hard not to dribble water all over her.

"We better get you to your room," Mom interrupts, obviously not hot on the idea of me bonding with Star. I can almost hear Mom's mind whirring, terrified by the thought that if I became friends with Star, I'd start borrowing her tops.

"I really am sorry," Star says, walking away. I mouth, "It's okay," and roll my eyes in Mom's direction. Star winks and smiles, then rushes away, having spotted her intended target.

"I still can't believe they put you in a coed dorm," Mom says nervously, watching Star pummel Marcus with a water balloon. I quickly bend down to pick up my soggy box so she doesn't see the smile on my face. Cohabitating with the opposite sex practically makes me a full-fledged adult. I can't give her any clue how excited I am about my new living situation or she'll yank me back to the minivan for another lecture about how sixteen is just too young to go away to college. And there is no way I'm leaving here. I shrug my shoulders and adopt a look of defeat so she thinks that I am just as distressed about coed living as she is.

I've been trying to disguise how excited I am all morning. It's hard considering I've wanted to come to McMillan College since I was twelve. That was the year I started competing in the state science fair that is held annually on campus. I fell in love with the old brick building that houses the most state-of-the-art science lab in the country. I couldn't get here to soak up all the unlimited knowledge soon enough. As last year's winner of McMillan's prestigious science fair, I won a four-year scholarship. Luckily, I had enough extra credits to graduate high school early. My dream is about to become reality. I know that Mom is proud of my academic achievements; it's just the moving away part that she isn't so jazzed about.

We make our way through the hallways packed with coeds hugging hello, exchanging numbers, and flirting shamelessly. I'm in heaven. Mom might soon be in need of a defibrillator because I don't think her heart can take much more. She's behind me muttering something about STDs under her breath. For some reason, Mom doesn't think I'm ready for college yet. It took my dad and me all summer to convince her that I would be okay on my own. After much pleading, I reminded her that I would only be forty-five minutes from home and so busy with the science club that I won't have time to get into trouble.

She's always been a little overprotective. To the point of social asphyxiation. I never wanted to worry her, so I didn't participate in many high school extracurriculars. I came to college to learn more and push myself intellectually, but getting away from Mom's stranglehold on my social life won't be a bad thing either. I know she means well, but I still need to make my own decisions.

"Here it is," I shout, unable to control the volume of my voice upon finding my dorm room door. This moment is the culmination of all my hard work the last sixteen years. I close my eyes, take a deep breath, and savor this monumental moment. No more obnoxious little brother, no more unchallenging high school classes, no more interruptions while I study. From now on if I want to go on a twelve-hour study binge, I can. I won't have someone bugging me to eat or rest my eyes. I am officially the boss of myself. I hear Mom impatiently shifting the box she is carrying on her hip.

I open my eyes and fling open the door to my new life while exclaiming, "Home sweet home."

Unfortunately, the weight in my box shifts just enough to throw off my already limited balance. The wet box collapses and my clothes go toppling into a heap in the middle of the floor, with my granny panties landing on top. I'm so focused on shoving my pathetic underwear back into the soggy box that the naked people on the bare mattress don't really register in my brain until I hear Mom scream. She drops her box and goes running down the hall. I just stand there, granny panties in hand, staring at the naked couple in shock.

"Are you Grace Kelly?" the naked girl asks, unflustered. She is stunningly at ease even though I just barged in on her having sex. She smooths her chestnut curls behind her ears, then props herself up on her elbow underneath the guy, who I just noticed has a very large dragon tattoo on his left buttock. I can't stop staring at it.

"I said, are you Grace Kelly?" the girl repeats. I hear her, but it's like I've been transported to another world. I've never actually seen a boy naked. I Googled the word "penis" once, but I chickened out and slammed my laptop shut before I could see any results. Hopefully he won't get up because I think I would pass out if he did.

"Stop checking out my boyfriend's ass," she shouts. I jerk myself out of my trance to see her smiling while he nuzzles her neck. She seems so sophisticated that I can't help but wonder what she is doing in the freshman dorm.

"Yes, I'm Grace Kelly Cook," I say, holding out my hand. The girl just giggles without reaching out to shake my hand.

"Those are hot," the guy says, laughing at the panties in my outstretched hand. I jerk my hand into my pocket to hide them.

"Don't be a dick, Aaron," the girl says, smacking her boyfriend on the butt. "I'm Jentry," she says, her striking green eyes apologizing for Aaron's comment. Her boyfriend is still pretty much laughing in my face. I realize that I must look even more ridiculous than normal from the water balloon incident.

"Can you, like, give us a minute?" she asks. When I realize I've just been standing here, staring at them, I pretty much want to die of embarrassment. What kind of a first impression have I made on the girl who is going to be my roommate for the next nine months? My face burns as I quickly kick some of my clothes to the empty side of the room.

"Oh, sure. Sorry," I say, scurrying out the door. I pull it shut tight so that they can have their privacy. I lean my head back against the cold metal door and try to steady myself. I'm shaking from making such an idiot out of myself.

I guess the postcard of the half-naked guy she sent me this summer telling me she was backpacking across Europe, as a reply to my get-to-know-me letter, should have tipped me off that she was so mature. My letter to her had been a three-page dossier of my life and achievements (excluding my age) to date. She must have thought I was such a dork. And now I bust in on her having sex with her boyfriend. She's probably calling the housing office to request a room transfer right now.

That was so not how I envisioned meeting my roommate. I hope she isn't mad because I kept staring at her boyfriend's butt. They must be really serious to be having sex. I think it would be cool to have a boyfriend, but I'm not ready for all the sex stuff yet. It would be nice to be kissed though, just to know what it feels like. There are just some things that Google can't explain.

I make my way down the hall past the unfamiliar faces. I know that I should be introducing myself to people, but it seems like everybody already knows each other, so it's kind of awkward.

McMillan requires all incoming freshmen to arrive a week early to acclimate themselves. That means that these students just met each other, yet they look like they have been friends forever. I've always been a little lacking in the social-networking arena. I had hoped that with McMillan being a small university, you wouldn't have the typical cliques. I thought maybe I could be successful not only academically, but also socially. I don't have any illusions of grandeur about being named homecoming queen or anything; I just don't want to spend another four years only being known as the girl who throws off the grading curve. But no one seems to see me. I continue down the hall, dropping my eyes to the floor. This is why I've always preferred books to people.

Wait a minute. I'm going about this all wrong. I'm doing exactly what I did in high school. How can I expect to get different results when I'm not willing to reconstruct my hypothesis? I can't believe I haven't thought of this sooner. Almost everything in life can be applied to the steps of the scientific method. First, I have to ask a question, then I do background research, construct a hypothesis, test with an experiment, and analyze my results to see if my conclusion is true or false. I glance around the hallway and notice that the most obvious difference between myself and my fellow coeds, besides the fact they aren't soaking wet, is that they are more outgoing.

I've never been particularly good at approaching people. I don't want them to think I'm a total stalker, but I don't have much time to do background research right now. My hypothesis (which is always written as: If _____ (I do this), then _____ (this) will happen, is: If I am friendly and approach people, then the possibility of making new friends will happen.

It is time to perform my experiment and collect the data. "Hi, I'm Grace Kelly," I force myself to say to a blonde hanging a dry-erase board on her door. I subtly wipe my suddenly damp hands on my pants just in case she wants to shake hands. I know that perspiring is just the body's way of cooling itself down, but that doesn't make it any less embarrassing.

She turns around slowly and looks me up and down. "No, you're not," she says, slipping into her room and shutting her door in my face. A glittery star with the name Sloane flutters above her new message board. I resist the urge to defile the new board with an obscene message because that would just be immature. She reminds me of some of the mean girls at my old high school who took to calling me "Graceless" because of all the accidents I had. Lucky for me, they always wanted to copy my homework so they weren't ever too mean. So much for that hypothesis. You don't need to be a genius to analyze those results. But I'm not willing to conclude that my hypothesis is false. I definitely need to conduct more experiments with different subjects. Sloane's words still hang in the air, stinging my skin. I don't think I'll attempt another experiment until this one has had a chance to fade away.

I continue down the hall, sort of depressed. This day is definitely not turning out how I had imagined. My phone vibrates in my pocket. I don't even have to look at it to know that it's my mom calling to make sure I didn't get forced into a threesome. As if my life could ever be that exciting.

• • •

"We can't leave her here, Stan. She isn't ready," Mom pleads to Dad as I pile back into our minivan. We decided to grab some lunch and let Jentry have plenty of time to finish up.

"Marge, stop being so dramatic. Kids have sex. Whether you like it or not, it happens. Just because Grace Kelly's roommate is doing it doesn't mean she is going to. You underestimate your daughter," Dad says, then catches my eye in the rearview mirror and winks.

"Who'd wanna have sex with Grace Kelly anyway?" my little brother, Sean, snorts while elbowing me in the ribs.

"There are plenty of people who would gladly have sex with me!" I shout in my defense. Mom turns to Dad as if to say "I told you so." "Not that I would or anything," I add quickly.

"She's just so young," Mom stresses.

"You're right, Marge. Let's take Grace Kelly back home," Dad says, making my heart race. "She can attend community college, and then if she's really lucky, she'll be running the grill at Steak 'n Shake in two years." I try to catch his eye again to thank him for using reverse psychology on Mom but he's too busy navigating the dorm parking lot, trying not to make road kill of any coeds.

"You know I don't want to deny her this opportunity. It's just that she can be so naïve sometimes," Mom trails off.

"You know I can actually hear you," I smart off, deeply offended. "And I'm not stupid, you know," I defend myself.

"Oh, Grace, don't be so sensitive," Mom says, spinning around to face me. "Of course you aren't stupid. You're the smartest person I know. But there is a big difference between being book smart and being emotionally smart."

She is making no sense. Smart is smart. And you don't graduate high school two years early and get a full scholarship unless you are smart. I'm smart.

"I just don't want you getting in over your head," Mom says gently, clasping my hand.

"Chill with the drama, Mama," Sean pipes up. "It's not like Grace Kelly is going to be hitting keggers. The craziest thing she'll do on campus is close down the library." He snorts. I kick him hard. I've tried several times to convince myself how it is scientifically possible that Sean and I are from the same gene pool. My brain still won't accept it.

"Shut up, Sean," Mom scolds him. "Do you realize that you have never even spent a night away from us?" She asks, turning her attention back to me.

"It's not my fault you kept me sheltered," I yell.

"Sheltered? I used to beg you to make friends."

"That's not how I remember things," I say, turning to look out the window. The truth is that I don't ever remember being invited to stay all night with anyone, so it was a non-issue. I hear Mom sigh loudly.

"Just promise me that you won't try to impress people by doing things you aren't comfortable with. You are much younger than most of these other kids."

I really wish that she would stop reminding me of my age. I'm not exactly going to be volunteering this information at freshman orientation.

Mom suddenly lunges toward me, her body wedged in the middle console. She places both her hands on my cheeks and makes me look her in the eyes.

"Just promise me," she says passionately. "Promise me you won't drink, do drugs, or have sex."

"I promise, Mom. I promise not to have any fun in college."

Sean doubles over in his seat, laughing. The corners of Dad's mouth are upturned in a smile matching mine. Mom gives me a disappointed look and slumps back down into her seat. Very slowly, I uncross my fingers.

• • •

When we get back to my dorm room, the door is standing wide open. I take it as a good sign that Jentry didn't throw all my clothes into the hall. I peek inside to see all of my clothes are folded and placed neatly on my bed. Jentry is taping several black and white photographs over the desk that she has chosen as hers. Mom clears her throat loudly, causing Jentry to spin around. She comes barreling toward me at the speed of light. My first instinct is to run; I figure she's mad that I was staring at her boyfriend's butt, but my feet won't move, and I'm holding my laptop bag in one hand and my bookbag full of reference materials in the other, so I wouldn't escape very fast anyway. But instead of pummeling me when she reaches me, she throws her arms around me in a giant hug. I just kind of stand there because I can't hug her back with all this stuff in my hands. Besides, I'm not really all that familiar with friendly displays of affection.

"It's so good to finally meet you," she says, releasing me and backing into the room so my family can come in.

"Yeah, you too," I say, surprised. It's almost like she doesn't remember what happened earlier. I won't be reminding her.

"Well, Jentry, you look really different with your clothes on," Mom says sarcastically. I give her a dirty look, warning her that she better not try to sabotage my newly formed relationship with Jentry.

"Sorry about that," Jentry says, shrugging. "I thought Aaron had locked the door."

"Will your boyfriend be visiting frequently?" Mom prods, setting my TV on my empty desk.

"Marge," Dad warns, smiling uncomfortably at Jentry. To my surprise, Sean is the only one who doesn't pipe up, but one glance at him tells me he is much too busy trying to imagine Jentry naked.

"It's okay," Jentry says, totally unfazed by Mom's attitude. "We were just saying goodbye. We broke up. He's staying back home and long-distance relationships just don't work for me."

"How would your mother feel about the way you said goodbye to Aaron?" Mom asks. She's like a Rottweiler after a steak when she's on a mission. I have a bad feeling that I'm going to be making a trip to the housing department once this conversation is over. We all stare anxiously at Jentry, waiting for her response.

I watch as her whole demeanor changes. Her tiny shoulders slump forward and her curly chestnut-colored hair falls over her face. When she finally looks up, her hair is still covering one of her startling green eyes. I can't get over how pretty she is. Our housing arrangement obviously wasn't based on looks. Her lip starts to quiver slightly as she answers.

"I guess she wouldn't be very proud of me," she says quietly. Sean slumps down on my mattress that is covered with shadows of old stains, obviously disappointed that Jentry isn't a total slut after all.

"Probably not," Mom says, almost beaming she's so proud of herself. "You probably wouldn't like it very much if I called her up and told her about it, would you?"

"Mom…"

"Marge…"

Dad and I both yell over each other. Why does she always have to take everything so far? It's like she wants to ruin it for me. Sometimes I almost think she's jealous of me and just trying to hold me back from things that she can't do. But that's crazy. She's my mom. How could a mother be jealous of a daughter?

"It's okay," Jentry says calmly. "I really wish you would call her, Mrs. Cook. I'd love to talk to my mom."

Mom tilts her head to the side and raises an eyebrow, not sure how to take Jentry's comment. Is she calling Mom's bluff or does she really not care if her mom finds out she was having sex?

"Because she's been dead for ten years," Jentry continues, shocking us all.

"Oh, you poor dear. I'm so sorry," Mom says, rushing to Jentry and throwing her arms around her. Jentry wraps her arms around Mom and returns the hug. After a few seconds, Mom releases her and studies Jentry's now tear-soaked face.

"I think your mother would be very proud of you, Jentry," Mom says, trying desperately to backtrack from her earlier statements. I feel bad for her. She can be a bit over the top sometimes, but she would never knowingly hurt someone's feelings.

"Thanks, Mrs. Cook," Jentry answers, wiping her face. "Do you have more stuff, Grace Kelly?" she asks, suddenly brightening.

• • •

After three trips to the minivan, and two trips to the first-aid kit (both for me), we finally got all my stuff to my room. Mom immediately opens one of my boxes and starts putting stuff where she thinks it should go. Couldn't she just ask me where I want my socks to go? Mom would just laugh at me if I told her that I Googled "feng shui" and I know exactly where to place my things to bring the maximum amount of harmony to my new life. She just wouldn't get it.

"You don't have to do that, Mom," I say, hoping that I won't have to spell it out for her.

Mom refolds a towel she pulled out of the box, then sets it gently on the bed. She glances around the tiny cinderblock room and sighs.

"Okay, I get it," she says, admitting defeat. She hugs me tightly and kisses me on the forehead. "Thanksgiving isn't that far away," she says, more to comfort herself than me.

"It'll be here before you know it," I say, praying that it isn't true. Dad comes up behind us and wraps his arms around both of us.

"Both my girls are going to be just fine," he says, kissing my cheek. I'm suddenly overwhelmed and it takes every bit of inner strength I have not to start crying. What is going on? I should be ecstatic that I am minutes away from being on my own. I've been counting down to this day since I got my acceptance letter. I'm ready to be challenged by harder curriculums. I'm ready to separate from my parents and annoying sibling. I'm ready to live with a total stranger. But what if I'm not? I think, panicked. What if Jentry is just putting on an act for my parents and doesn't like me at all? I grip my parents tight, trying to squeeze out some of my fear.

I sneak a peek over Dad's shoulder to see Sean checking out Jentry's butt while she puts away her clothes. She turns around and busts him. She smiles and he blushes. I see her slingshot something across the room to him and when he jams a pair of thong panties into his jeans pocket, I'm not sure if I should scream in horror or fall down laughing. Jentry sees me and smirks, and all of my fear evaporates because I know we are going to get along just fine. I also can't help but wonder if maybe Jentry is the variable that might help me prove my hypothesis true.

• • •

Jentry and I spend the next few hours setting up our respective sides of the room. Her side is completely covered with black-and-white photographs, expensive-looking bedding, and stylish accessories. My side is filled with my many dictionaries, encyclopedias, and some old textbooks I thought I might need for reference. I thought about setting my new trinocular compound microscope out but I was afraid somebody might break in and steal it, so I tucked it carefully away in my sock drawer. Nobody would ever think to look there. The only personal photo I have propped up on my desk is one of Sean and me last Christmas.

"GK, you're a minimalist when it comes to sentimentality, that's for sure," Jentry laughs.

I beam at her, not because of the comment, but because she's only known me for four hours and she's already given me a nickname. I've never had a nickname before because that one in high school totally doesn't count.

I can't believe how quickly we've bonded. It's like fate brought us together. I didn't really have any girlfriends in high school. I was always too busying studying and I never really met anyone who understood me.

Jentry plugs her iPod into its base and one of my favorite songs comes blaring out of the speakers. I'm so comfortable that I start dancing around the room.

"I just love William," I say, throwing my hip out a little too far and catching it on the end of my desk. Ouch, that's gonna leave a mark.

"It's Will.i.am," Jentry replies, laughing.

"Huh?" I throw my butt out and wiggle it around to the beat. Jentry throws herself on her bed in a laughing fit. I'm starting to wonder if maybe I'm not as good a dancer as I imagined. Oh well, Jentry won't tell anyone. Our first secret. This is exactly how I pictured college!

I move to Jentry's side of the room to browse her photos. They are amazing. The photographer has captured the essence of the moment so well that I almost feel like I'm there.

"Wow, who's this?" I ask, pointing to a particularly striking photo of a woman swinging with her hair blowing behind her in a perfect sheet.

"That's my mom," Jentry says proudly.

"She's gorgeous. Who took all of these?"

"I did. I'm a photography major," she answers.

"But—"

"Yeah, she's not really dead. I was just messing with your mom," Jentry giggles. I stand rooted to the ground, unable to move. What kind of a person lies about their mom being dead? I wasn't sure, but I knew that Jentry was exactly what I needed to kick start my new life. I look over at her and start laughing. Before long we are both practically on the floor, squatting, so that we don't pee our pants we are laughing so hard.

"You know she's probably researching campus grief-recovery groups as we speak?" I tell Jentry.

"I couldn't help it. She was just such an easy mark. I can't imagine what you've had to endure," she says, panting heavily from laughing so hard. She falls down on her bed and the expensive comforter swallows her small frame.

"She's not that bad. I mean, as far as moms go," I say, suddenly feeling guilty laughing at Mom's expense.

"It's okay, GK. I'm not saying she's Satan or anything, but did you pick those pants out for yourself?" she asks, reaching over to pull on my elastic waistband. "I thought you had to have an AARP card to buy anything like that."

I pull away from her and move over to my own bed. I ease myself down on my old Disney Princess sheets and comforter. The truth was I grabbed the pants from a rummage sale pile my grandma brought to our house. Mom begged me to wear something different and even gave me money to go clothes shopping. Instead, I took it and bought my new microscope. Mom was not thrilled but I convinced her I needed the microscope much more than I needed aesthetics. After a few weeks, she finally stopped trying to take me shopping. Now I can't help but think that she may have had a point. I've always thought of clothes and shoes as frivolous, but maybe I should just consider them more variables that can be used to help prove my hypothesis true.

"Hey, I didn't mean to offend you. It's just that in your letter this summer you said you wanted to make some changes," she reminds me.

She's right. For once in my life, I'm going to be making my own decisions. I can do whatever I want, and I'm going to, starting right now.

"Let's go get something to eat, like pizza, or something really bad for us," I say, jumping off the bed.

"Now you're talking," Jentry replies ecstatically.

• • •

"So, were you and Aaron having sex?" I ask Jentry, immediately cramming more pizza into my mouth, and gazing at the old photos on the walls to avoid meeting her eyes. We're sharing a booth in a pizza place on campus. From the looks of the photos, this place has been a favorite hangout for at least forty years. I love the idea that I'm sitting in the same booth as several generations of college students before me. One photograph catches my eye and I do a double take, realizing that the pants I'm wearing are almost identical to the ones the woman in the forty-year-old photo is wearing. I'm not loving that.

"No, we were playing doctor," Jentry responds, laughing

into her plastic cup of beer. I was too chicken to order one myself. I was terrified they would ask to see my ID. Then they would embarrass me in front of Jentry when they found out I was only sixteen. I know I should be honest with her about my age, but I'm just not ready yet. They never even carded Jentry. She exudes such an air of confidence that no one seems to question her. I imagine that she must go through her entire life feeling the way I did at my Scholastic Bowl tournaments. I was always so confident. It would be really cool to feel that way all the time.

"Was he, you know, your first?" I ask, getting back to Aaron. I roll the cool outside of my soda glass against my cheeks to control the blushing brought on by the memory of Aaron's dragon tattoo.

"My first what? On campus?" she laughs, picking off a piece of pepperoni and popping it into her mouth. "Wait a minute. Are you a virgin?" she asks, her eyes huge.

I contemplate lying, but I figure I'm going to need a lot of help from Jentry if I'm going to navigate the waters of college better than I did the ones of high school.

"Yeah, I am. It's pathetic," I confess, dropping my face.

"No, it's not, and don't let anyone tell you that it is," Jentry says forcefully, surprising me.

"You really don't think it's pathetic?"

"What? That you respect yourself enough to keep it until you're in love? Not hardly," she smiles, going back to picking off her pepperoni. "In fact, I think it is so un-pathetic that just to show my solidarity, I'm going on a boy strike. Besides, who needs boys when we've got each other?"

"That's really sweet, Jentry, but I'm sure you'll make more friends," I say, touched by her comment but not dumb enough to believe that she'll spend her time hanging out with me once she meets other girls.

"Of course I'll make more friends, and so will you, but we're roomies, so that means we'll be best friends," she says, smiling so genuinely that there is no way I could ever doubt her.

"I've never even kissed a boy," I confess, not the least bit worried that she'll make fun of me.

Her head pops up and she drops her slice of pizza. "Now that is pathetic," she laughs. "Stick with me, GK. This is going to be the best year of your life."

I smile and go back to eating my pizza. Move over, Grace Kelly. GK is here to stay.

TWO

"I'm so psyched about my classes," I tell Jentry, as we haul our new textbooks back to the dorm.

"Sometimes you say the weirdest things," she laughs, readjusting her heavy load on her shoulder.

"Do you need to rest a minute?" I offer, realizing that in my excitement I'm losing Jentry. I am still buzzing from picking up my first official class schedule. I swear I almost screamed when I found out that I had tested well enough on my entrance exams to be placed in a sophomore chemistry class. I stop to let her catch up, taking the opportunity to wipe my glasses off on the tail of my button-down oxford. They are fogged up from leaving the air-conditioned paradise of the bookstore and moving into the ninety-degree day. God knows I'm dangerous enough when I can see.

"Yes, please," she laughs, collapsing under an oak tree

on the quad. I put my bag down and slowly ease myself down. I'm wearing a jean skirt of Jentry's that she let, or more like insisted, I borrow. I think I was five the last time I wore a skirt, so I'm hoping I don't accidentally flash somebody.

"My parents are going to be excited when I call and tell them my books were only three hundred dollars. We had five hundred budgeted," I say.

Jentry grabs my hand and stares deep into my eyes. "GK, you never, ever tell your parents the real amount you spent on books. It's the cardinal rule of college. That's two hundred dollars you could use for new clothes or whatever you want."

"I don't lie to my parents," I say, pulling my hand away from her.

"Fine, keep wearing granny panties and elastic pants," she mutters, fanning herself with a spiral notebook.

I grab a hold of my thick mane of hair and pull it into a ponytail using a rubber band. It is so hot today that it doesn't even make a difference. I glance longingly at Jentry in her tank top and short shorts.

"Stop staring at me, freak," she laughs.

"Do you think I'd look okay in a shirt like yours?" I ask her, pulling on my blue oxford that has zero ventilation.

"Not as good as me, but then again who would?" She cracks herself up again. I pull a notebook out of my book-bag and start to fan myself like Jentry. I turn my head to study the other students on campus. More upperclassmen are arriving every day, but campus is still pretty sparse.

Some students are listening to their iPods while downing bottles of water, others are making out in front of everyone, others are just like us, trying to escape the brutal heat while hauling a hundred pounds of books back to their dorm.

"I could use a beer right now," Jentry says, wiping the sweat from her brow.

"I wouldn't turn down an iced tea," I reply, cringing when I realize how immature my choice of beverage must sound to Jentry.

"Waiter, one Bud Light and one iced tea, please," she jokes, flagging down an imaginary waiter. She doesn't seem to care one bit that I didn't want a beer.

"I can take our books back to the dorm if you have other stuff to do," I offer. I can't help feeling that Jentry is taking pity on me by spending so much time with me. Surely she will want to start making friends with other girls soon.

"Are you trying to ditch me?" she asks, clutching her chest dramatically.

"Of course not. I think it's really sweet that you've been spending so much time with me, but I know you are probably ready to meet some other people."

"Did it ever occur to you that I really like you?" she asks, her eyes bugging out.

Actually, it hadn't. It's not that I don't consider myself likable. It's just that people like me and people like Jentry don't usually intermingle unless there is a lab or class project involved. As much as I would like to change the way people see me, hanging out with Jentry isn't going to magically do that for me. They might put up with me if I was Jentry's friend, but I want people to like me for me.

"I know you do," I finally answer. "But I'm not sure you'll want to spend your weekends the way I do."

"You can get good grades and have a life, you know," she says matter of factly.

I had figured out the good grades part; it was the life part I was having trouble with.

"I can help you," she says, reading my mind.

"Why?" I ask bewildered. I wouldn't be one bit surprised to see a camera crew jump out from behind one of the quad's oak trees to tell me I've been chosen for some new reality show where a cool girl mentors a geek.

"Why not?" Jentry replies, so genuinely that I don't want to jinx it by questioning her more.

"How?" I can't fathom how Jentry thinks she can reverse sixteen years of social awkwardness, but I am willing to try if she is.

She doesn't say a word, but points toward the middle of the quad. I notice a group of freshly glossed, perfectly tanned girls strutting toward us. I can't concentrate on their almost seemingly synchronized movements because my eyes focus in on the huge letter *A* they all have on their pink tanks tops.

"What did they do?" I ask Jentry, mortified for them. The posse of modern-day Hester Prynnes don't look like they are being publicly ostracized; actually, it is quite the opposite. Everyone who crosses their path is smiling and waving, but I still feel that they must have done something horrible to be marked with the *A*s.

"They're Greek," Jentry explains dreamily.

"Huh," I grunt, confused. I always thought people of Greek origin were dark-haired and dark-eyed. I would have guessed these girls to be of Swedish or Norwegian descent.

Jentry looks like she drank a bit too much of her imaginary beer. Her eyes are glazed over and for a minute I'm afraid she might be suffering from heat exhaustion. Then I follow her eyes and can almost feel myself getting sucked in right behind her.

The five girls stop right in front of us. One of the girls hands me a blue piece of paper, then extends one to Jentry. I'm too awestruck to thank her. I'm not sure what it is that has me so completely spellbound. All five of the girls are striking, but none of them are prettier than Jentry, although I guess I could be biased. They just seem to travel inside this vortex of campus celebrity. There isn't a person walking by that doesn't take notice of them. I wonder what it would feel like to have people look at you that way. To be worshipped and revered.

"Hi, we're the Alphas," the pixie-looking girl that handed me the flier says. "And we want to invite both of you to rush in a few days."

"Hope to see you there," they all singsong in unison before trotting off in a perfect V formation.

"Oh my God! Those were the Alphas, the best sorority on campus," Jentry exclaims, clutching her flier with a death grip.

"What's a sorority?" I hate it when I don't know the answer to something. Jentry turns to look at me, an amused look playing on her face. She obviously thinks I'm joking until she sees my clueless expression.

"Seriously?" Jentry asks, astounded. "Oh my God, GK. You have lived such a sheltered life."

Like she has to remind me.

"A sorority is a social organization of women who unite for sisterhood," Jentry explains. "Ah, who am I kidding? They are a bunch of really cool chicks who get together and party for four years. Oh, and they do lots of philanthropy and stuff, too," she laughs.

"Oh."

"And the Alphas are *the* best sorority on campus," Jentry clarifies.

"How do you know all of this?" I ask, amazed.

"My friend's sister from back home was a Delta Zeta at Southern. She taught me all about Greek life."

"So what's 'rush'?" I ask, glancing down at the blue paper the Alpha sister gave me.

"Rush is the process you have to go through to be selected by the sorority. It's not really the same here at McMillan because they only have two sororities and we definitely don't want to rush Zeta Sigma Alpha. Every chapter on every campus of that sorority is bad news." I nod my head like I have some idea what she's talking about, even though nothing could be further from the truth.

"I don't really think those girls would have any use for me unless their GPAs need a boost," I say, shoving the flier into my bag of textbooks. I can always use it for scratch paper.

"Stop whining, GK. They'd be lucky to have us," she says, her eyes gleaming.

"Oh, no. There is no way I'm going to humiliate myself like that."

"You asked me earlier how I could help you get more of a life. GK, this is how," Jentry stresses, shaking the flier in front of my face.

"But I don't know the first thing about this stuff."

"You know stuff about cold fusion and I know stuff about the hottest sorority on campus. I'll help you."

I don't bother telling her that I don't know the first thing about cold fusion because I can tell there is no way I'm going to talk her out of this. And when I start envisioning a house full of girls that are as close as sisters, I'm not sure I want to talk her out of it. Jentry is right—if I really want to make some changes, there is no better way than to rush the Alphas. Once I make the decision that I'm actually going to do this, I'm so excited I feel like I'm about to burst, which I know isn't scientifically possible, but it still feels that way.

"I want to be an Alpha," I proclaim, jumping up. My foot gets tangled in my bookbag and I slam back to the grass, my legs sprawled out for the world to see my granny panties. I hear a whistle from somewhere close by.

"Oh, man. We've got our work cut out for us," Jentry says, helping me up.

• • •

"What is wrong with your face?" Jentry cries out as she barges through the door.

I run to the mirror expecting to see that I've broken out in hives or something, but it's just me staring back at myself. Well, not really normal me, but me amplified a bit.

"What?" I ask, inspecting my face. "You don't like it?" I sort of borrowed some of Jentry's fancy makeup. I've never used makeup before except a little bit of blush, but I Googled "how to apply makeup" and I think I did a pretty good job. I didn't understand why some of the results kept saying that people shouldn't be able to tell you are wearing it and it should look natural. I want people to know I'm wearing it, so I put it on twice as thick.

"You only have three eyelashes," Jentry points out, gesturing toward my over-mascaraed lashes. "Let me guess. Google?" she asks, laughing.

I drop my head and nod numbly, embarrassed that I thought I actually looked good.

"GK, you've got a serious Google fetish. You have to understand that sometimes you just have to practice things before you can perfect them," she says, pulling a wipe out of a plastic dispenser. She starts wiping the excess makeup off my face. Her comment cheers me up. She is absolutely right about practicing. My freshman year in Biology 101, I went through five frogs before I finally figured out how to dissect one correctly. After a couple more attempts with the makeup, I should have it mastered.

"How about for real-life stuff, you ask me? I'll be your real-life Google. You're gonna have to keep Googling that science crap, though, because I don't know squat about that," she laughs.

"Thanks, Jentry. I've never had a friend like you before," I say, tearing up but forcing myself to hold back so my layers of mascara don't run.

"Don't go getting all sappy on me," she says, winking. "I take it the makeup experimentation has something to do with rush?" I nod, hating that I'm so transparent.

"Listen, GK. I think you are perfect just the way you are, but if you really want to make some changes, I can help you," she offers.

"Will you really? That would be so awesome," I squeal.

"Beauty can be painful," she says grabbing my shoulders. "And I don't want to hear any whining," she adds forcefully.

"Yes, ma'am." I salute her, jumping around the room excitedly.

"We don't have much time," she suddenly realizes. She grabs the campus phone book and starts flipping through it like a maniac. She stops on a page, grabs her cell phone out of her pocket, and frantically dials a number.

"Yes, we need your geek-to-chic package, ASAP," she mumbles into the phone. A few seconds later, she clicks off, grabs my arm, and pulls me out of the dorm.

• • •

"You're sure you want to do this?" the stylist asks me, holding a pair of scissors under my ponytail.

"More than anything in the whole world," I reply. My head starts to jerk a little as she saws through my thick stump of hair. A few seconds later, I feel five pounds lighter. "Make sure you save that so I can donate it to Locks of Love," I tell her, not looking up. I want to wait until my highlights and cut are completely done before I look at myself. I should have done this years ago. I can't help but wonder why Mom never tried to talk me into cutting my hair more stylish or why she never taught me about makeup.

"Holy crap, GK. She shaved you like an alpaca," I hear Jentry say. I can't see her, only her hand, which is holding a Diet Coke.

"Very funny. Aren't you supposed to be finding me some rush clothes?" I ask, gesturing wildly for a drink of her soda. I try to sip it upside down but the soda just runs into my nose, making me sneeze.

"About that. This little excursion isn't going to be cheap, you know."

I had forgotten all about paying for this stuff. Of course, I've been saving for college since I was eight, but that money has to last four years. I can't be blowing it all the first week. But surely a hairdo and some basic cosmetics can't cost that much.

"How much are we talking?" I ask Jentry.

"About four hundred for your hair and makeup," Jentry says nonchalantly.

"Dollars?" I yell, jerking my head up. My stylist calmly pushes it back down and continues cutting the long layers that Jentry requested.

"I told you, beauty is painful," Jentry says tapping her foot impatiently. I guess I did promise no whining, but how can these people sleep at night charging such astronomical prices for the use of scissors and hair dye? I have two hundred extra from my book savings and I'll pay for my new clothes out of my savings. That leaves me with two hundred more that I need to come up with.

"Jentry, hand me my phone," I say, gesturing toward the corner of the stylist's vanity.

She doesn't say anything, but hands it to me under my hair. I take a deep breath before dialing my parent's phone number. Sean answers on the second ring.

"I already moved into your room," he boasts, obviously making use of the caller ID.

"Nice try, troll, but I know Mom wouldn't let you do that," I laugh. The truth is she is probably praying for me to come running home to her any day now. Nothing would make her happier than for me to call and say I couldn't cut it away from her. I'd rather eat glass.

"I'm really glad you're gone," he teases. "The extra attention I'm getting from Mom is really super," he says, his voice slightly bitter.

I feel a small tinge of guilt, but not enough to distract me from the reason I called.

"You'll live, Sean. You know what they say. What doesn't kill us makes us stronger."

"They never met our mom. She started making me wear my helmet again," he says disgustedly. I don't have the heart to tell him that I actually agree with Mom on this one. I've seen Sean's report cards and he is one head injury away from repeating eighth grade.

"I need to talk to Dad," I say, choosing the lesser of two evils.

"No can do, sis. They went on a date."

"With each other?"

"I know. Creepy, right?"

It is a little out of character for my couch-potato parents. I don't dwell on it though because I am too excited that I don't have to actually talk to them and can make Sean do my dirty work.

"I need them to deposit two hundred dollars in my checking account," I tell him. "Write this down so you don't forget," I insist.

I hear him rummaging through our junk drawer for a pen and paper.

"Grace Kelly needs two hundred dollars for a giant box of condoms. Got it," he howls, cracking himself up.

"Thanks, Sean. Bye," I say, wondering why my mother is always so worried about me when her other child is so clearly in need of help.

"Bye, sis. Oh, and tell that sweet honey of a roommate of yours that I've got a special place for her panties," he laughs, clicking off.

I fight the urge to throw up in my mouth as I flip my phone shut.

. . .

"How much more of this do I have to endure?" I whine, tired after a day of being waxed, tweezed, highlighted, and exfoliated. Who knew beauty would be so time consuming? I was really hoping to get some advance reading done for some of my classes, but at this rate it isn't going to happen today.

"Shut it. I told you, no whining. Besides, as soon as you put this vest on, you'll be done," Jentry replies, with a huge smile on her face. I know I must look pretty good the way she's been grinning all day, but I haven't seen myself yet. Jentry thought it would be more fun if I waited until after she'd done my makeup and I'd changed into one of my new outfits. I know I feel different, in a good way. I like the way my hair swishes around my shoulders every time I move. I caught a glimpse of the highlights when I was attempting to put in contacts for the first time, even though Jentry had my hair wrapped in a towel. I could see a bit of auburn, which I really liked.

I pull the vest over the short-sleeved silk shirt I'm wearing.

"Careful, GK," Jentry shouts, running over to help me slide the vest over my head. "Don't mess up your hair."

"You sure are taking this seriously," I joke, adjusting the vest over my shirt.

"Hey, when I start a project I take it very seriously, and I have a feeling that Project Geek to Greek is going to be my biggest accomplishment yet."

"Hey, I wasn't a total geek," I defend myself, even though I know she's right. I'm smart enough to know that looks aren't everything, but I'm not dumb enough to believe they don't matter at all. Besides, I wasn't happy with the way I looked. I made Jentry believe that the makeover was only for the Alphas, but mostly, it was for me. I've never been comfortable in my own skin.

"Here put these on," Jentry says, thrusting a pair of black heels at me.

"Oh, no. I can barely walk in tennis shoes," I refuse.

"Just try them on in here. You don't have to walk any-where. I just want you to get the full effect of the outfit," she insists. I grab the shoes from her and slip them on, instantly adding three inches and lots of wobble to my height.

"Smile," Jentry says, grabbing her phone to take my picture. I try my best not to look awkward like I normally tend to in photos. She snaps a few pictures, then lays the phone back on her desk. I get sort of melancholy wishing I could email a picture home to my parents. But my mom would be on her way to pull me out of school within an hour, claiming I had already succumbed to the peer pres-sures of college and that makeup and hair products are just gateways. She'd swear that if I kept up this pace, I'd be using a flat iron and getting a Brazilian (I just found out what this is today, and Mom would never have to worry about me doing that) by Christmas.

"Are you ready?" she asks, nearly bouncing with excite-ment.

I nod and turn to face the full-length mirror on the back of our dorm room door. Jentry pulls down the white sheet she had up and, at first, I think there is a stranger in the room. Very carefully, I walk up to the mirror. I put my hands into my shiny, reddish-brown layered hair. I keep touching it, not believing that this is the same hair I've spent almost my entire life pulling into a ponytail each day. The next thing I notice are my eyes. I can actually see them without my glasses covering them up. Jentry lined them in a deep violet liner and used a very light brown on my lids to make them stand out even more. Each of my lashes look a mile long, coated perfectly in black mascara. My cheeks and lips are the same exact shade of pink. I stare down at the outfit I'm wearing, which looks tailor-made to fit my body. Jentry was right about the shoes; they look amazing with the dress capris I'm wearing. Who knew I had legs like this?

"Well, what do you think?" Jentry finally asks, still bouncing up and down in excitement.

"Is it really me?" I ask, unable to take my eyes off myself.

"It's the upgraded version of you," Jentry laughs.

"It's me. It's really me," I say, dancing around with excitement. I grab Jentry's arms and start flinging her around. I lose my footing and twist my ankle, throwing my whole body off balance. I drop Jentry's hands before I go flying to the ground, landing on the hard concrete floor with a thud.

"See, I told you it was still you," Jentry laughs, helping me to my feet.

Later that night, Jentry corrals all the girls on our floor to go to dinner. Until now, Jentry and I have mostly stayed to ourselves, so none of the girls have a clue about my make-over. For the first time in my life, I feel confident about not only my brains but my appearance, too.

There are six of us seated at a round table covered with a red-and-white checkered tablecloth. We have mostly been discussing classes, which finally start in a few days, and I cannot wait. There is nothing more exciting than opening a pristine notebook and filling it with exciting new facts. I am glad that the university insists on incoming freshmen moving in a week before classes start, though. It has been great spending so much time getting to know Jentry and now no one on campus will know me as geeky Grace Kelly. Here, I'm just GK.

I plan to spend most of tomorrow routing out the quickest way to get to each of my classes so I don't take the chance of running late and missing one ounce of lecture time.

"So, Grace Kelly, what's your major?" a chunky girl with ebony hair asks me, interrupting my trailing thoughts.

"I'm pre-med. I want to be a pediatrician someday," I answer confidently. I've known that I wanted to be a doctor since I was twelve and Sean brutally severed one of my dolls limbs with his baseball bat. I had so much fun fixing her up that I ripped her other arm off on purpose.

"Cool. It must feel good to know what you want to do

with your life. I don't have a clue," she says, taking a sip of her iced tea.

"I'm going to open my own photography business someday," Jentry pipes up before sticking a cheesy nacho in her mouth.

"She's amazing. You guys should see her pictures," I brag.

"Maybe you could do some sorority headshots for me," Sloane says. If she has any recollection of our first meeting, if you can call having a door slammed in your face a meeting, she doesn't show it. She tosses her long, straight blonde hair over her shoulders. She's so tan she must have spent the entire summer someplace exotic. I'm no label connoisseur, but even I can tell that all of her clothes and accessories are designer. She probably sweats money. I can't stop myself from imagining what her life as a rich, beautiful girl must be like. I'm hoping that she was just having a bad day the first time we met. I realize I'm gawking and quickly avert my eyes, but not before noticing that she has at least one flaw. Her fingernails are bitten down to the quick. It takes everything I have not to break into a lecture on the millions of germs lurking under our nails, but something tells me she wouldn't appreciate it. Besides, it's kind of nice knowing she isn't completely perfect.

"What sorority are you in?" I ask her. Maybe she is one of those people that you really have to get to know to appreciate their personality, I think, giving her the benefit of the doubt.

"I'm not, officially, but soon I'll be an Alpha," she answers, not bothering to look up at me.

"That's really cool. Jentry and I will be rushing the Alphas too," I say excitedly.

"You're going to rush the Alphas?" Sloane asks, finally looking up. She has this really weird look on her face, like I've just told her the funniest joke imaginable.

"Yeah, she is. Do you have a problem with that?" Jentry blurts out before I can answer. I look over at her to see that her cheeks are flushed and that she's holding her fork more like a weapon than a tool to eat with.

"To each his own," Sloane shrugs. "Just remember, a haircut and some lip gloss doesn't change your entire personality." She laughs and points to my chest. I look down to see that I've dripped marinara sauce all down the front of my new white blouse. I try to blot at the sauce with a napkin, but I just end up smearing the entire front of my shirt with sauce. Suddenly the idea of trying to become an Alpha sister seems completely ridiculous. What was I thinking?

"Hey," Jentry says and tosses her balled-up napkin at me. "She's just jealous of you."

"That's right. I'm jealous of a girl who should still be wearing a bib," Sloane laughs.

I don't know what comes over me. Maybe it was the torture of my first eyebrow waxing at the spa, or maybe it was because I basically embezzled money from my parents for a makeover, but before I know it, I take my spoon, dip it in marinara sauce, and launch it toward Sloane. It splatters perfectly on her light pink dress. All of the girls start laughing and Jentry nearly falls out of her chair.

Sloane sits stunned for a few seconds. When she finally looks up, her eyes sear into me. As good as throwing the sauce at her felt, my knees start to shake in fear at seeing her face now. I can't believe I just did that! I've gone my entire life flying under everyone's radar and now I've just pissed off the meanest girl on campus.

"You are so going to pay for that, geek." She bolts out of her chair and takes off out of the restaurant.

Her words etch themselves in my mind. Could she be right? Will the Alphas just look at me and laugh? Will all these changes still result in my hypothesis turning out false?

"Don't let her get to you, GK," I hear Jentry's voice whispering to me. I smile falsely and nod, knowing she already has.

• • •

"Let's watch a movie," Jentry says. She busies herself looking through her DVDs while I take a stain remover stick to my new blouse. I still can't shake the things that Sloane said tonight. I've never had anyone be so deliberately mean to me before. But then again, I've never thrown marinara sauce on anyone before either.

"How about *The Breakfast Club*?" I hear Jentry ask from far away.

Sloane was right about one thing. This stain proves that I'm still the klutzy girl I was before the new clothes, makeup, and haircut. I'll never be able to look as poised and sophisticated as the Alphas, no matter how hard I try.

"Okay, what about *Pirates of the Caribbean*?"

I've already lied to my parents and gotten into a food fight with a girl who lives two doors away, probably making myself an enemy for life, and for what? So that I can show up at rush and completely humiliate myself? The Alphas will probably laugh me off their doorstep.

"Hmm ... what about *Willy Wanker and the Fudge Packing Factory*?"

"What?" I shout and spin to face Jentry.

She's sliding a DVD into the machine, laughing. "I thought that might get your attention."

"Are we really watching a ... a—"

"A PORNO!" Jentry screams. "I thought you might need a little pick-me-up."

"I can't. I won't," I say, pacing the floor of our dorm room. I'd be a total liar if I didn't admit to being a little curious though. I sneak a peek at the screen but it's still black.

"Chill out, GK. Come take a load off," she says, patting the empty side of her bed.

"Don't you think this is kind of weird?" I ask, moving slowly to her bed.

"What? Two chicks watching porn together?" She looks at me for a second with a completely straight face, then starts cracking up. "It's not really porn," she says, gesturing toward the screen.

She hits *play* before I can catch the name of the movie, but I'm already breathing easier knowing it isn't porn. I definitely want to become more worldly, but I don't need to learn everything my first week at college.

Actor credits start flashing on the screen and I'm surprised to see Cary Grant's name followed by Grace Kelly's.

"*To Catch a Thief*?"

"I thought you might need a little reminder that you aren't so different from your namesake after all," she says, turning up the volume. "Don't you listen to any of that crap that Sloane said tonight. The Alphas would be lucky to have you."

I'm touched beyond belief that someone who has only known me for three days would know exactly how to make me feel better. Mom and I used to watch old Grace Kelly movies every Sunday. I can't remember why we ever stopped.

"I think your mom was really on to something when she named you," Jentry says looking from me to the television screen.

It's the nicest thing anyone has ever said to me.

THREE

Rush is here already. My brain knows that it is impossible for any forty-eight hour period to be longer than another, but my rush preparedness time seems so much shorter than the two days I had to go without Internet access because of a snowstorm. I have never been this nervous before. I even tried mentally reciting the table of periodic elements alphabetically, my surefire way of beating the physiology of nervousness, but even that didn't work.

"I don't know about this," I whisper to Jentry as we wait to enter the Alpha house.

"It's going to be fine. Just be yourself," she says, winking.

Doesn't she know that's what I'm afraid of? That I will be myself. Klutzy, socially awkward, sixteen-year-old Grace Kelly Cook.

But wait—no one here knows that girl. I keep forgetting

that until I prove them otherwise, I'm just another incoming freshman trying to impress them. I can do this. Besides, Jentry explained that rush at McMillan is very informal; the two sororities each host a get-to-know-you party. And since Jentry assured me that we don't want to be Zetas (I didn't admit it to her, but I Googled them, and not only are they skanks, per Jentry, but they also have an embarrassingly low GPA average), that just leaves the Alpha party to attend.

Surely I can manage to avoid an accident and make interesting conversation through one party. Beyond that, it's pure statistics. The Alphas will pick the girls they like the best, then narrow their choices based on the number of spaces available in the sorority. Even if I'm a borderline choice, my GPA should push me over (the Alphas take their academics seriously).

I take a deep breath and smooth down the outfit Jentry picked out for me. I'm wearing a navy blue sweater and a pleated plaid skirt with ivory-colored tights to hide all my bruises. The last thing I need the sisters thinking is that I'm some domestic violence victim. I even mastered the art of walking in kitten heels, although I have no idea why they are called that. Jentry and I have role-played hours of witty banter. I prepared for rush just like I would any important test, except this time I used makeup, styling products, and pop culture as study guides. I'm ready to rip open my test booklet and start filling in circles with my number two pencil, metaphorically anyway.

I'm starting to feel normal again until I glance around at my competition. Girls are hurriedly fluffing their hair and reapplying lip gloss; some look almost as nervous as me as they continuously wipe their palms against their designer outfits.

I do a quick mental count of the girls in line. Thirty-three. So thirty-three girls vying for, wait, I just realized that I never asked Jentry how many pledges the Alphas could pick. I sure can't figure out my probability of becoming an Alpha without that critical piece of the equation.

"Hey, Jentry? How many girls will the Alphas pick?" I ask her.

She looks around wildly, and if I didn't know better, I'd think she was thinking of making a break for it.

"Um, I don't know?" she answers.

My nervousness has just hit a new plateau. Actinium, Aluminum, Americium, Antimony, Argon. I fidget with the name tag on my sweater just for something to do with my hands. I have to admit I am glad that Jentry talked me into using my full name for rush instead of the nickname she gave me.

"How many?" I ask again, the familiarity of the elements calming me.

"Two," Jentry blurts out, cringing like I might hit her.

"Do you know that I have a better chance of having a stroke? Right here. Right now."

"Grace Kelly, don't do this to yourself," she warns, uncharacteristically calling me by my full name.

"What if they don't like me?" I whisper. Jentry rolls her eyes at me. I wish I could have the confidence that she has.

She is the only girl here who isn't sweating profusely or beating herself up emotionally.

"Everybody likes you. You're impossible not to like." She smiles back at me.

"Sloane doesn't like me," I remind her, glancing over at the bronzed, blonde-haired beauty.

"Sloane is an evil Barbie-clone and the Alphas are going to see right through her," Jentry says, catching Sloane's eye and flipping her off. Sloane immediately throws me a death look and I quickly avert my eyes. Something about that girl really scares me.

"I guess you're right," I say hesitantly, still remembering Sloane's comment at the restaurant.

A loud foghorn sounds, interrupting my self-esteem crisis, and all of the girls throw their hands to their ears. The large white door to the Alpha house is suddenly thrown open to a foyer and staircase decorated like a cruise ship. The Alphas stand at attention in crisp, white uniforms and navy captain hats. One by one, they come and take a prospective pledge by the arm and escort her into the house.

Jentry gives me a wink and a half-wave as a redhead with two long braids hanging down from under her hat escorts her into the house. I stand up straight with a smile plastered on my face, trying not to faint as each prospective pledge disappears into the house. I feel beads of sweat forming on my forehead. Waiting to be picked by an Alpha is the sorority equivalent of playing Red Rover when I was in elementary school. The other team never picked me because I was, and still am, so clumsy.

Sloane breezes by me in a cloud of expensive perfume, escorted by a pixie-like Alpha with short black hair and wide blue eyes. Her hat practically swallows her entire head as she walks by, giggling something to Sloane. I nearly throw up as I realize that I'm the last one standing with no sign of an escort. All of the other prospective pledges are standing inside the foyer with their Alpha escorts, watching me. I try to do a quick physics problem in my mind of how fast I could possibly run in kitten heels without killing myself.

A shadow falls across the foyer. I look up to see one of the girls I remember from the Alpha posse I first saw on the quad. She is almost as tan as Sloane, with shoulder-length, curly blonde hair. She is the only Alpha wearing a white skirt with her uniform instead of pants. I also notice some patches on her shoulders that I assume indicate her elevated Alpha status. She smiles and seems to float over to me.

"Hi, I'm Lindsay Landry. Welcome to the Alpha Alpha Alpha house," she says sweetly as she hooks her arm into mine and starts leading me into the house.

"The sorority so nice, they named it thrice," I chuckle nervously.

"That's funny," Lindsay laughs.

"I'm Grace Kelly. I was starting to freak out a little bit being the last one picked and all," I confess, immediately wanting to duct tape my mouth shut.

"We always save the best for last here at the Alpha house," she says, putting me at ease. My nervousness quickly melts away but I still focus on walking very carefully. The last thing I need tonight is to fall down and make an idiot out of myself.

"So, have you been an Alpha for long?" I ask, making small talk.

"Ever since I got here three years ago. This is my first year as president, though, so this year is even more special." She beams as I glance over to make sure I heard her right.

"You're the president of the Alphas?"

"Yep." She smiles at me like she didn't just drop a huge bombshell. I was already worried about impressing the Alphas, but now I have to impress *the* Alpha? How in the world am I going to pull this off? We approach the door and I see Jentry smiling brightly as she puts an index finger up to each corner of her mouth. My fear must be showing. I remember to paste my smile back on as we reach the threshold.

How is it that I can memorize a quantum theory in twelve seconds but I can't smile and walk in heels at the same time? My foot gets caught on the threshold and I fall hard on the Alphas' pristine marble foyer, nearly taking Lindsay with me. I feel a sensation of skin splitting, which I am all too familiar with. I try to get up as several girls rush to help me, but I can only see out of one eye and nearly fall again.

"GK, you're bleeding," Jentry says, digging through her purse. She finds a tissue and presses it against my left eyebrow. Something tells me that I won't have to worry about getting my eyebrows waxed again for a while.

The girls huddle around me with mixed looks of sympathy, revulsion, and pity on their faces. My eye is throbbing but the pain doesn't even compare with the hit my pride took. I should have known that this was a mistake. I'm never going to be some sophisticated girl that everyone on campus looks up to.

"Alphas, take your pledges into the talent show," Lindsay commands, taking charge. Slowly, the crowd files into another room. I see Sloane hold her thumb and index finger into an *L* and giggle before she disappears.

"Let's get you cleaned up," Lindsay says, pulling me to my feet and taking me into a bathroom at the back of the house.

She eases me down on a closed toilet and starts rifling through a medicine cabinet.

"You don't have to do this. I could just leave," I say, trying to spare her from having to cut me loose later. I'm sure it's pretty obvious that I'm not cut out to be an Alpha.

"What? You think a little scrape is going to scare me off?" she laughs. "Check this out," she says, lifting her skirt above her knee to reveal a large scar. "Freshman year. The Alphas had a hayride and I fell off the hayrack. Look at this one," she says, unbuttoning her shirt part of the way and slipping a tanned shoulder out. A faint scar of at least ten stitches runs through the middle of her perfectly toned shoulder blade. "Diving accident, Alpha pool party, my sophomore year. Wanna see more?" she asks eagerly.

"No, that's okay," I laugh. She starts dabbing a cotton ball saturated with first-aid wash on my cut. It stings like crazy but I force myself to hold still.

"Everybody thinks the Alphas are so perfect, but we're not. We're just regular girls that are lucky enough to be in a very special sorority. Why do you want to be an Alpha, Grace Kelly?" she asks, unwrapping a bandage.

I'm a little taken aback by her question. I mean, three days ago I wouldn't have known an Alpha from a Zeta. But now that I do, I guess I can't imagine not being a part of something so unique. All the other extracurriculars I've joined in the past have been a bit tainted by too much testosterone (science club, debate team). Bonding with other girls is really important to me now, especially after having so much fun with Jentry.

"I've always been really good with grades, but not with people. I really want college to be different. I want to belong to something really special for once. And for some reason, I just know that I belong here," I answer truthfully.

She stops wiping my cut and smiles at me.

"Good answer," she replies, putting the bandage on my cut. "Good as new," she says, washing her hands. I stand up carefully and survey myself in the mirror.

"Oh my God," I yell. The bandage is so big it covers all of my left eyebrow and part of my lid. Lindsay spins around, splattering my sweater with her wet hands.

"What's wrong?" she cries.

"I look like a pirate, and not in the good Johnny Depp way," I say, putting some of my new pop culture knowledge to work. I would cry if I wasn't afraid the bandage adhesive would go in my eye and blind me for good.

"You look fine," she laughs, trying to dry off my sweater with a hand towel.

There is a knock on the door and Lindsay opens it. The Rho Chi, Marjorie, steps in and notices the bandage. She doesn't bother to hide her laughter. Rho Chis, I've learned, are sorority sisters who unaffiliate themselves from their sororities until rush is over. They are responsible for guiding the prospective pledges through rush without showing preference for anyone. Marjorie is a terrible Rho Chi. I overheard her say that the Alphas are an inferior sorority. I don't think she even knows what the word means.

"Come on, pledge Cook. It's time to join the party," she says, taking me by the arm.

"Thanks, Lindsay," I say, trying to keep up with Marjorie without tripping again. She drags me into a room holding a piano and nothing else. I can hear laughter coming from the front of the house.

"Listen, Grace Kelly. I know this was an accident, but if anything else happens, I'm going to have to pull you from rush. I can't have you being an embarrassment," she says, and then storms off. I stay in the room for a few minutes catching my breath. My stomach is still tingling from being alone and actually having a conversation with the Alpha president. Lindsay is so nice, and made me realize that the Alphas aren't going to pass me up just because of one little accident.

I follow the laughter into an elaborately decorated great room. I've never been on a cruise before, but I can't imagine anything more closely resembling a lido deck. My mom would completely love the creativity that the Alphas put into decorating. She is constantly filling our house with new decorations that she copies from Martha Stewart. A pang of guilt hits me in the gut, but dissolves just as quickly when a sorority sister shoves a tray of fruity drinks garnished with pineapple wedges toward me.

"Would you like a non-alcoholic piña colada?" she asks sweetly.

"Thanks," I reply, delicately taking a glass from her tray. She flitters off as I take a long sip. I try to look nonchalant as I sip, trying to figure out how I'm going to infiltrate the little cliques of girl-chatting that formed while I was getting patched up.

"Are you okay?" Jentry appears by my side, looking worried.

"Never better," I lie.

"Nobody thinks anything about it, GK," Jentry tells me, resting a reassuring hand on my shoulder. She directs me over to a group of girls and introduces me.

"You're so brave. I would have been crying like a baby if I cut myself that bad," an Alpha named Constance says.

"Head wounds always bleed more, so it looked way worse than it really was," I reply. I can't tell if the girls are dazzled by my knowledge or completely grossed out, but I feel better anyway.

Our conversation easily flows from classes, to instructors, to dorm food, to boys. Pledges and sisters interchange groups until I'm positive I've talked to everyone here. I can't believe how nervous I was to meet the sisters. Everyone is so nice.

"Grace Kelly, that is too funny," Leah, an Alpha, says after I finish telling them about Jentry slingshotting Sean her thong on move-in day.

"Your little brother sounds like a bigger pervert than mine," someone adds.

"What did I miss?" Sloane giggles, joining our group. She's been putting on quite the act tonight, but I know the Alphas must see through it. I hope so, anyway. I still can't help but be paranoid that she is going to try and ruin this for me because I threw sauce on her.

"Grace Kelly was just telling the funniest story," a sister says.

"Grace Kelly is quite the comedian. She had everyone cracking up over dinner the other night," Sloane agrees.

I did?

"You two know each other?" Leah asks.

"We're practically neighbors at the dorm, aren't we?" Sloane says sweetly, draping her arm around me. She seems so genuine that I can't help but wonder if this is her way of saying she wants to start over. I know I do.

The sisters offer to take us on a tour. Sloane smiles easily at me as we follow them up the stairs. I catch Jentry's eye and she doesn't look as eager to befriend Sloane quite yet. We follow the sisters up the stairs to the bedrooms. I can't help but fantasize about how great it would be to call this amazing house my home. It would be a bit tricky keeping it secret from Mom. I didn't exactly mention rush to her during any of the ten phone conversations we had in the last two days. I knew she would just assume that I was too young and would think that the Alphas would be a bad influence on me. It would be cool if she could see how sophisticated I've been tonight, minus the eye-patch bandage, of course. I think she might have even been proud of me if the circumstances were different. Jentry is so lucky. She never has to report to anybody. Her family doesn't even call.

Our tour is over and the other girls file back to the great room. I duck into the bathroom to check on my newest scar.

At least I didn't need stitches, I think, making my way out into the hall. The hallways are covered with giant picture frames of past Alphas. I stop and look at a few of them, daydreaming about my photo being in a frame hanging on these walls some day.

"Jesus, you look like something out of a horror movie," I hear Sloane's voice say from behind me. I spin around to face her and stumble a bit. I don't know if the spin knocked me off balance or if it was the look on Sloane's face. The girl who was chatting so amiably alongside me just a few minutes ago is long gone. The girl in the hallway is the same one I threw the pasta sauce on.

"I'm really sorry I threw the sauce on you, Sloane," I say, hoping she'll accept my apology. After all, we could be in the same pledge class soon.

"Oh, you're going to be sorry," she says, reaching out and shoving me. I fall back against one of the picture frames. It dislodges from the wall and crashes to the floor in a million pieces. I jump away just in time to avoid being cut by the shattering glass.

Active sisters and rushees quickly flood the hallway. My face starts to burn until I realize that this wasn't really my fault, and the Alphas will understand that when they see Sloane. I look to my side, but Sloane is gone. The only thing the Alphas see in the hallway is me, standing among shards of broken glass, and their prized picture frame in a thousand pieces.

"It was an accident," I say. With Sloane not around, no one is going to believe a story about me getting shoved, so I don't even bother.

Marjorie shoves through the crowd and takes my arm. "That's it. I'm removing you from rush as a safety hazard to the other pledges." She drags me back down the hall to the front door.

"GK, wait!" Jentry yells, rushing up behind me. "I'll come with you," she offers, half-heartedly.

As much as I wish that things could have turned out differently, I'm not about to deny Jentry her happiness, even if, selfishly, I would love for her to leave with me.

"No, you stay. I want you to," I say, smiling at her. Several of the sisters wave forlornly at me.

"Are you sure?" she says, as Marjorie pulls me out the door. I flash Jentry one last fake smile to make her think I'm okay.

• • •

"You left me no choice," Marjorie says, letting go of my arm for the first time since we left the Alpha house.

"It wasn't my fault. There's this girl and she's got it out for me. She shoved me into the picture frame," I say, praying that Marjorie will change her mind and take me back to the Alpha house. She looks at me and shakes her head.

"It's over, Grace Kelly. Go home." She turns and heads back to the Alpha house without even giving me another glance. How could she be so cold-hearted?

"Can't you just give me another chance?" I yell to her retreating figure. She doesn't even bother to look back. Once Marjorie is completely out of sight, it hits me that my future as an Alpha is really over. I start to cry, loudly, knowing that the darkened quad is abandoned.

"It's all because of these stupid shoes," I scream, kicking the heels off. "I hate these shoes," I continue screaming, scooping them up off the ground. I throw one of the shoes as hard as I can and hear it bounce off a neighboring tree. I throw the other shoe then collapse to the ground, crying.

"Jesus," I hear a voice say, about a millisecond after I hear the second shoe hit something. "Are you trying to kill me?" The voice comes closer and I look up, through my tears, to see a guy rubbing his forehead with one hand, and holding my shoe with the other. I think about jumping to my feet, trying to save some face, but then I figure this is probably the worst day of my life and I really don't care what some random stranger thinks of me.

"Does this belong to you?" he asks, holding my shoe out.

"If I say yes, are you going to press charges?" I ask, sniffling.

He laughs and holds a hand out to help me up. I stand up and face him.

"I don't think you are supposed to cry for at least two days after having Lasik surgery," he says, suddenly serious.

"Huh?" I ask, confused, until it dawns on me. The eye patch/bandage from hell. There is definitely no face to save here. This is definitely the worst day of my life.

He laughs, still holding my shoe out to me. I grab it, drop it, and against my foot's protest, shove it back on.

"I'm kidding, by the way. Hey, are you okay?" he asks when I don't respond to his joke, which was funny, but I just can't bring myself to laugh after tonight's catastrophic events.

"Yeah, I'm fine. Thanks," I say, standing all cockeyed with one shoe on and one off.

"Where's your other shoe?" he asks, looking down at my feet.

"I don't know. I think maybe I wounded an elm over there," I say, pointing in the direction that I heard the shoe hit.

"I'm gonna go out on a limb and say you're not a tree hugger, are you?" he laughs. "Go out on a limb, get it?" He starts cracking up and I can't help but let out a few giggles against my will.

He trots off in the direction that I pointed, and after a few seconds, he comes back looking happy, holding my other shoe. He bends down in front of me and slips it on my foot.

"Do you think Cinderella tagged Prince Charming in the head with her shoe before he slipped it on her foot?" he laughs, getting to his feet.

"I highly doubt it and I don't remember Cinderella ever wearing an eye patch either," I grumble. He runs a hand through his curly brown hair that's damp with sweat. The neck of his T-shirt is also ringed with sweat and I notice an iPod velcroed to a sizable bicep with ear buds trailing down his chest. His T-shirt has a large horseshoe looking emblem on it. I recognize it as the Greek symbol for Omega. Memorizing the Greek alphabet is the only learning I've done on campus so far. That must mean that he belongs to a fraternity, which almost brings on another flood of tears. I suck them back, focusing instead on his face. It's too dark to see what color eyes he has, but I can make out the deep pit of a dimple in his left cheek every time he laughs. He's adorable in a never-gonna-get-him-so-don't-even-bother-drooling kind of way. So what's he doing standing here being nice to me?

"I'm Charlie Miller. Do we know each other? You look familiar," he says, crinkling his brow while studying my face.

"I don't think so," I reply curtly, turning away. He is making me blush by staring at me so hard. Only it's not in a creepy way, it's like he really thinks he knows me. I almost giggle when I realize how absurd it is that an adorable frat boy thinks he knows a big science geek like me.

"Wait a minute. You won the McMillan science fair last year, didn't you?" he says, beaming with joy that he placed me.

I don't even bother to hide my shock. I'm completely mortified that my super-duper makeover obviously isn't so super-duper after all if Charlie can recognize me, in the dark no less.

"It is you," he exclaims. I nod my head in agreement. "You were the talk of the science department last year. There were some XY science majors who had a hard time losing out to an XX high schooler. Present company excluded, of course."

I am dangerously close to passing out thinking that Charlie is going to remember that not only was I a high schooler, but technically, I was only a sophomore. Thankfully, he doesn't show any sign of remembering my exact age.

"I'm kind of a science geek," I admit, laughing uneasily.

"Hey, there's nothing geeky about science. I should know. I'm a chemistry major," he laughs. "So, do you know what your entry in the science fair is going to be this year?"

So that's what this is all about. He's trying to hijack my science fair idea that I haven't even had a spare minute to think about yet.

"You're good," I smart off. "Who sent you? Was it Rashee? You can tell him that I'm going to cream him just like I did last year. Tell him my entry is going to be even more amazing than it was last year," I bluff.

Charlie's eyes get huge and he backs a few steps away from me. "Wow, even better than the French-fry oil-powered lawn mower, huh? Well, good luck."

How in the world did he know what my entry was last year? There was a tiny write-up in the local paper and my dad does still tool around the yard on it. Then he started craving McDonald's every time he rode it, so my mom made me convert it back to regular gas.

"Wait, you aren't a spy?" I'm such a dork. I hit the guy in the head with my shoe. How in the world could he be a spy sent by my science fair competition?

"Actually, I was flirting with you, but obviously I need to work on my game a bit," he says, looking mortified. He slips in his ear buds, flashes me a smile, and takes off running before I've fully grasped what he just said.

A cute frat boy hitting on me? Clearly, I have not become acclimated to the new-and-improved Grace Kelly yet. Holy crap, a cute frat boy was hitting on me!

"Wait," I yell after him. "Sorry about your head. I'm Grace Kelly, or GK for short, by the way," I shout, hoping his music isn't up too loud.

"See ya later, GK for short," he shouts back from the dark shadows of the quad.

• • •

I've got to figure out a way back into the Alphas, I think to myself on the walk back to my dorm. But how? I practically begged Marjorie and she wouldn't budge. I know that the Alphas also hold rush in the spring semester, but that is too far away. I just can't wait that long.

"It's all because of these stupid shoes," I say, pounding them into the ground. It's actually Sloane's fault, but as much as I'd like to pound her into the ground, I can't, so the shoes will have to do. The campus is deserted with most everyone at rush, and once again I feel like the geeky girl not invited to the cool party. Angrily, I dig through my purse to find my ID so I can get into the dorm. I jerk it out, pulling out some maxi pads at the same time. I bend down to grab them before anyone can see when a hand intercepts mine.

"I'm not stalking you, I promise. It's just … cute girl, dark campus … not a good combo," Charlie says, handing me back a pad.

"Okay, this is officially the worst night of my life," I say, grabbing the pad from him and shoving it back into my purse. Did he just call me cute? I hope that he can't see that my cheeks are on fire.

"Oh, please. It takes a real man to pick up a feminine hygiene product," he laughs.

"It was really nice of you to look out for me," I say, trying my best not to lose myself in his dimple. "I'm really sorry about your head."

"I'll wear it like a badge of honor," he laughs, rubbing the bump on his forehead.

"Okay, see ya," I say, dragging out our goodbye.

"Yeah, see ya." He jogs off, waving.

I'm about to pull the door open when I hear him call my name. I spin around, hoping he's back to ask me out.

"Whatever it was that was bothering you, I hope it gets better." He winks and disappears, taking with him all the warm fuzzies from our flirtation. The nausea I felt earlier about being rejected by the Alphas comes rushing back as I remember how horrible my reality really is.

• • •

I get back to my dorm room and exchange my skirt and sweater for a T-shirt and jean cutoffs. I can't stop thinking about the Alphas. Part of me wishes I had never heard of them so that I wouldn't be so miserable right now. I tell myself that I was fine before I met the Alphas and I'll be fine after meeting them. Besides, I'll still have Jentry. Oh my God, Jentry! If Jentry gets into the Alphas, and I'm sure she will, I'll barely see her. It would have been so perfect if Jentry and I had been the two girls the Alphas picked as their pledges. If only Sloane hadn't been waiting for me in the hallway. Things would have turned out so differently. If only I could figure out a way back in.

I grab my laptop and sit cross-legged on my bed. I boot it up and punch in the campus website URL. After a few clicks, I'm browsing the Alpha website. I've pretty much got it memorized after researching the Alphas the last few days. I click to my favorite page: the sisters all holding their elaborately decorated wooden pledge paddles and beaming proudly after last year's initiation night. I had imagined myself in the new picture so many times. Now it looks like the only way that will happen is if I Photoshop it in. It stings to look at, especially now, since I recognize so many of the sisters after meeting them tonight.

I go to Google and type in "Alpha." The search yields about a billion results, mostly of other Alpha websites on different campuses. I click through some of the sites and am met with more beaming girls proud to be Alphas. This is so incredibly unproductive. I'm about to slam my laptop shut and order a large pizza to eat by myself when something catches my eye. I'm browsing the website of an Arizona chapter of the Alphas when I see a photograph of three women. The caption above the photo says, "Three generations of Alphas." An elegant, silver-haired woman and a middle-aged brunette have their arms around a younger blonde. Underneath the picture it says, "Legacy Ball 2007, charter member Francine Dougal with her daughter, Joy, and granddaughter and legacy, Jill."

I go back to Google and type in "sorority legacy." I click on the first result, which explains that a legacy is the female descendent of a sorority sister. It says that if someone in your family has been a member of a sorority, the sorority must give the heir preferential treatment when she rushes. While legacies are not given as much weight as they once were, most sororities will still honor the former sister by accepting her heir into the house.

Marjorie never said a word about legacies when she explained the rules of rushing to us. According to this, if I'm a legacy of the Alphas, they pretty much have to take me. There's only one problem. No one in my geeky family has ever even come close to rushing. I can't believe I found a way in only to be shot down again.

I quickly Google "Alpha" and "McMillan College," just to see if fate is possibly on my side. The way I see it, if I'm meant to do this, I'll find something. And if not, I'll give it up and resign myself to a non-Greek life. After an excruciating millisecond, Google turns up three results. I click on the first one, which is a website for a cosmetics company called Edwina Fay. I scroll down, wondering if Google is losing its magic touch, when I see a tube of lipstick to click on for Edwina's bio. I click on it, and it brings up a pink page with a huge photo of a beautiful, although heavily made up, woman. I read through Edwina's bio, hardly believing that she is the same age as my mom; she looks like she could be twenty. Edwina attended college at my university in 1978. She was an Alpha the entire time she went to school here. I scroll down to see that in addition to marrying several times, Edwina goes on to say that she has two brothers, two nephews, and a teenage niece whom she dotes on. Jackpot!

I quickly Google "Edwina Fay" and "niece," which yields no results. I try Google images, but there are still no results. I do several more searches to try and dig up information on Edwina's niece, with no luck. So, Edwina Fay has a teenage niece and there is absolutely no trace of her on the Internet. This could only mean one thing. This is totally meant to be. Oh. My. God. I found a loophole into the Alphas, and Edwina Fay is her name.

FOUR

I don't even take the time to change back into my rush clothes. I ignore my ringing dorm phone as I slip on a pair of tennis shoes and grab my purse, and before I know it I'm back in front of the Alpha house. Unfortunately, the adrenaline rush I was being fueled by ran out about half-way across campus. Now all I'm feeling is pure fear.

Can I really lie my way into the Alphas? Surely they have people to check stuff like this and they won't just take my word for it. The idea of being busted by the Alphas makes me nauseous, but not nauseous enough to turn around.

I pound on the door with my fist. To my surprise, Sloane throws it open. Her million-dollar smile falls when she sees it's me. The foyer behind Sloane is empty and the frenzy of excited voices that filled the house earlier is gone. This can only mean one thing. The Alphas have already picked their pledges, and Sloane is one of them.

"No one here ordered any geek, so why don't you run along," she hisses, moving to slam the door in my face.

"Pledge Masterson, who told you that you could answer the door?" Lindsay's voice booms from behind Sloane. She comes into view holding a Diet Coke.

Pledge Masterson? Hearing Lindsay's confirmation of Sloane's new status in the house makes me want to hurl. How can the Alphas not see how horrible Sloane is? It seems I'm too late to try and get into the Alphas. They already have their two pledges. I should just turn around and go back to my dorm before I make an even bigger fool of myself. But I don't. My feet stay rooted to their spot; it's almost as if they too know they belong here.

"What are you doing here, Grace Kelly?" Lindsay asks curiously.

"I forgot to tell you something earlier," I say, kicking the threshold nervously with my tennis shoe.

"Come on in," Lindsay says, holding the door open. I slide into the foyer, quickly realizing how underdressed I am. Lindsay doesn't seem to notice my thrown-together outfit.

"We're not mad about the picture frame, Grace Kelly. Accidents happen. Marjorie was out of line for pulling you from rush," she says, surprising me.

"She was?"

"Definitely. The Alphas gave you full consideration when choosing our new pledges. But…" She tosses her blonde hair over her shoulder nervously, obviously not wanting to finish her sentence. "Our quota is two pledges, and there were thirty-three prospective pledges. It was really tough to choose this semester. I'm sorry, Grace Kelly, but you didn't make the final cut. We chose Sloane and Jentry." My heart lifts a bit to hear that the Alphas chose Jentry.

I hear a snicker come from down the hallway and I don't need to guess who it is. Won't Sloane be surprised when the Alphas make an exception for a third pledge?

"Lindsay, there's something I forgot to tell you earlier," I say, biting on my lower lip to keep it from quivering. I haven't had much practice lying and it doesn't help that I'm starting out with a doozy like this.

Some of the other sisters start wandering into the foyer with curious looks on their faces. At least I think they look curious. Who can tell with this bandage over my eye? My palms are sweating as Lindsay stands there waiting patiently for me to tell her the biggest lie I've ever told. I nearly chicken out when Jentry rounds the corner with a mocktini in her hand. She beams from ear to ear when she sees me.

"I'm an Alpha legacy," I blurt out. Jentry's eyes widen and she nearly chokes on her drink.

"What do you mean?" Lindsay asks, clearly confused.

"My aunt, Edwina Fay Brighton, is an Alpha," I explain, hoping she'll get it this time because I feel like I might be struck down in this foyer if I have to repeat it again.

"Oh my God! Edwina Fay is your aunt?" the redheaded sister with the braids practically screams. She grabs hold of her uniform shirt and rips it open. The buttons go scattering across the marble foyer. "I love Edwina Fay," she screams, pointing to the T-shirt she is wearing underneath her uniform. My faux aunt's picture is plastered across the red-head's chest with the saying, "Edwina Fay is my home girl."

"Edwina Fay was one of the Alpha founders. She's the most successful Alpha in our history," Lindsay says, stunned.

And here I thought the lady had a quaint little makeup business. Great. Leave it to me to pick the alpha Alpha to be related to. I'm going to be so busted.

The other girls start to swarm around me. I'm getting dizzy only being able to see out of one eye.

"That's why your skin is so beautiful," a sister says, reaching out to touch my cheek.

"Could you get us a discount on makeup?" someone asks from behind me.

"Could we, like, meet her?" another asks, nearly making me faint.

What have I gotten myself into? When the Alphas find out the truth, I'll be laughed off campus. I'll be living back home enrolling in community college, sans stylish clothes and makeup, before the week is out.

"I'd love for you to be a pledge, Grace Kelly. But I thought the Alphas could only have two pledges?" Sloane asks so sweetly that her voice is practically dripping honey. In my nervousness, I hadn't seen her slither back into the room.

"This certainly changes things a bit," Lindsay says, clearly flustered. "Of course, I'm going to have to check things out with National tomorrow. The sisters and I are going to have a lot to discuss." She looks stressed and I feel bad for making this hard on her. She has been so nice to me.

National? This means that I have about ten hours before Lindsay finds out the horrible truth. What will she think of me when she realizes I lied to her? What if Jentry isn't allowed to keep rooming with me once the Alphas find out what a fraud I am? What have I done?

"It would be so fun having you on board, Grace Kelly," Sloane adds, interrupting my nearly full-blown panic attack. She immediately starts gnawing at her fingernails like they're corncobs. I still can't believe that such a perfect-looking girl has such a revolting habit.

"Legacies are given priority. So someone could lose their bid," Lindsay says ominously. I'm very careful to avoid Sloane's eyes as she spits a nail in my direction.

• • •

"Holy shit, GK. You just told the mother of all lies. You realize that, right?" Jentry whispers as we sit side by side on her bed. We're being very covert just in case Sloane has her ear plastered to our door, which I wouldn't put past her. "I'm so proud of you," she says, grabbing my shoulders.

"Why? For being a big fake? That's nothing to be proud of," I say, the guilt from my lie finally kicking in.

"This is huge. You went after something you wanted. You didn't care if somebody told you that you couldn't have it. Of course, you're going to crash and burn like nobody's business tomorrow after Lindsay calls National, but for a few brief hours, you're every geeky girl's hero," she finishes, getting a little misty eyed.

"Gee, thanks. I think." I try not to think about tomorrow, but my stomach starts churning remembering Lindsay's request that we all return to the house at eleven in the morning.

"You might have actually pulled if off if you wouldn't have picked the CEO of the most successful cosmetics company of all time. Oh God, I can't stand it. GK, you should do stand-up." Jentry dies laughing while rolling off her bed.

"How in the world would I know anything about makeup? I just wore eyeliner for the first time three days ago," I point out in a useless defense. Nothing I say is going to stop the fit Jentry is having. Despite my nervousness over my demise with the Alphas, I can't help but realize the irony of the legacy I chose. Couldn't I have just looked at one more Google search? I start cracking up just watching Jentry roll around on the floor holding her stomach.

"So, I met a boy today," I say after she has finally calmed down a bit.

"Ooh, do tell. Is he hot? Well hung? Come on, give me details," she laughs.

"Well, it was dark, but he looked really cute. I hit him in the forehead with my shoe," I giggle.

"NO!" Jentry screams with laughter. I nod and she just starts cracking up all over again.

"Then I saw him again later and he helped me pick up the maxi pads I was carrying in my purse," I laugh.

"He actually picked up a pad?" she asks, amazed.

"Yeah."

"He's totally into you. Guys are scared to death of feminine hygiene products; it's like their kryptonite. Yep, he's into you."

I hear something outside our door and I jump off the bed and put my finger to my mouth, gesturing for Jentry to be quiet. I am so going to bust Sloane for spying on us. I fling open the unlocked door, ready to pounce.

Instead, I practically headbutt a portly campus security guard standing outside our door with his fist raised, ready to knock.

"Are you Grace Kelly Cook?" he asks grumpily.

Did the Alphas change their mind and decide to have me hauled in for breaking their picture frame? Did Lindsay already figure out that I lied?

"Yes, I'm Grace Kelly." I smile, hoping to win him over.

His stubble-covered face doesn't register any emotion. He pulls a black walkie-talkie off his shoulder and speaks into it. "The subject is accounted for," he says.

"Ten-four, Bob. Tell her to call her mom so she quits calling campus security," another male voice crackles out of the walkie-talkie.

Bob raises his eyebrows unpleasantly at me and stalks off down the hallway. I shut the door and crumple into a ball of humiliation onto our dorm floor.

"Your mom gives new meaning to the word controlling," Jentry says, half-laughing.

"I can't believe she called campus security. She's on a mission to destroy me no matter where I go." I shake my head while dialing my home phone number.

I calm Mom down by lying and saying that I slept through both phone calls. There was no way I was going to tell her about rush. She'd probably call in the National Guard. I made her promise to never call campus security again or I wouldn't come home for Thanksgiving break. We bartered over how many times a day she could call. She finally settled on one call a day but unlimited emails. Jentry sat shaking her head and laughing through the whole conversation. I'm positive she thinks my entire family is whacked because her mom hasn't called her once since she's been here. I ease myself down onto my covers and turn myself in Jentry's direction. She has her hair fanned out on her pillow with just one of her iPod ear buds in.

"I bet your family really misses you," I say, trying not to be too obvious.

"Highly unlikely," Jentry responds, pulling out the ear bud.

"What are they like?" I prod.

"The polar opposite of your family," she says, rolling over in her bed.

"You say that like it's a bad thing," I laugh.

"You're really lucky, GK. I know it doesn't always feel that way, but you really are."

Her comment is laced with such sadness that I don't know how to respond. How could her family not completely treasure her? I know I do.

"Besides, you're my family now," she says, flipping back over.

"Sisters," I agree. I can't believe how close I've gotten to

Jentry in just a few days. I almost can't imagine college without her. And I know that no matter what happens tomorrow, she'll be there for me.

I'm nearly asleep when a bolt of panic runs through my body. What if, by some insane chance, I get into the Alphas, but it also causes Jentry to get kicked out?

FIVE

The next morning, I'm sitting next to Jentry around the cherry wood dining table at the Alpha house. I'm so nervous that my knees are knocking against the bottom of the table and all the other sisters keep looking around, trying to figure out where the noise is coming from.

"Just be cool," Jentry whispers, gently laying her hand on one of my legs.

She's right. What's the worst that can happen? Oh, that's right. I could become the laughing stock of the entire campus when Lindsay reveals that I lied about being a legacy. I don't even know why I came here. I should run back to the dorm as fast as I can and never leave my room again. I move to get up just as Lindsay walks in. The whispering from the other sisters ceases immediately. I scoot around in my chair trying to get as comfortable as possible. I might as well enjoy the last precious moments I have left in the Alpha house.

I wonder if the Alphas would have more respect for me if I just stood up and told the truth? Lindsay clears her throat before I can muster the courage to speak up.

"Good morning, everyone," she begins. "I'm very happy to announce that we do not have to say goodbye to either of the pledges that we so carefully chose last night."

Jentry clasps my hand for support as all of the sisters look at me with confused looks on their faces. Sloane looks relieved and immediately pulls her fingers out of her mouth. She will love it when Lindsay reveals to the other sisters that I lied.

"I'm also ecstatic to welcome a new pledge," Lindsay babbles excitedly. Jentry squeezes my hand as Lindsay's words make it from my ears to my brain. The route is much slower than normal this morning. "Sisters, please welcome our newest pledge, Grace Kelly Cook."

Cheers erupt all around the table as I sit stunned. How did this happen? Jentry reaches in to hug me and the moment our eyes meet, I know. The secret phone call she placed this morning. At the time, I thought it had something to do with her family. But now, I have no doubt, she single-handedly made it possible for me to be an Alpha. I squeeze her until she squeals.

"The woman at National just couldn't get over how nice your aunt was," Lindsay brags. "I think she was a little star struck."

"She gets that a lot," I say, finally letting go of Jentry.

"Maybe she can come visit some time," Lindsay says, looking hopeful. I smile at her, forcing myself to enjoy this moment and not stress about how I'm going to pull off the next four years.

"Okay, girls," Lindsay shouts. "Let's celebrate in style." Two active sisters come in carrying boxes of Krispy Kremes and gallons of milk.

Jentry raises her plastic cup of milk to mine in a toast, throwing me a sly wink as a sister attaches a pink-and-gold pin to my collar. I try to focus on the compliments and congratulations that are coming my way, but I can't seem to focus on anything but the tiny circle-shaped pin on my collar. It has a white background and is edged in gold with three overlapping pink capital *A*s in the middle. I've always been proud of the *A*s I've received before, but these are by far the ones I'm the proudest of. I run my fingers gently along the edge of it.

"You're going to rub the gold right off that thing," Jentry teases me.

I drop my fingers self-consciously and whisper, "I can't believe you did this." She holds a finger to her pursed-out lips, but her eyes crinkle up in a smile.

"Okay, girls. I need your attention," Lindsay says, taking a seat at the head of the table. A sister grabs the empty doughnut boxes from the middle of the table so that we don't have to struggle to see Lindsay.

"It is time to explain to our pledges what is expected of them," she continues. "I'm sure you already know this, especially if you visited the Zeta house, but the Alphas aren't your typical sorority. We don't believe in belittling or humiliating our pledges through hazing. But that doesn't mean that we won't test your loyalty to us. Loyalty, above all else, is what makes us sisters."

The active sisters clap in agreement while Jentry and I exchange a fearful glance, wondering how we'll be asked to prove our loyalty.

"The three of you," Lindsay says, addressing Jentry, Sloane, and me, "will be expected to complete The Alpha Bet before your bids, or offers of sisterhood, become active."

I tap Jentry on the hand underneath the table to see if she has any idea what Lindsay is talking about. She shrugs her shoulders, looking clueless.

"The Alpha Bet is a set of twenty-six alphabetical tasks chosen for you, by your fellow sisters, to prove your loyalty to the sorority."

It doesn't sound so bad, but I can't help but notice how serious all the sisters suddenly got. How hard could these tasks be anyway? I've already lied to get here, and there isn't much I wouldn't do at this point to go from geek to Greek.

"I'm passing out sheets of paper with your letter on them," Lindsay tells the actives, getting up to distribute the papers. "Because there are more than twenty-six sisters, not everyone will get to choose a task for each pledge. I have tried to divide the letters as fairly as possible."

The sisters clutch their papers to their chests, making Lindsay's next statement no big surprise.

"No one is to discuss their tasks. Not with each other or outsiders. Do you understand?" The three of us nod our heads like obedient bobbleheads.

"Three sets of letters will be hung in the great room. When you complete a task, the letter will be removed. This is so the other sisters can gauge your progress. We know that if being an Alpha is what you really want, you will find a way to succeed."

Jentry and I raise our eyebrows at each other and let out tiny sighs. Suddenly this sisterhood business seems like really hard work. And to think that classes haven't even started yet.

• • •

After Lindsay's revelation, I barely had time to go to the bathroom before I was approached about my first task. These sisters don't mess around.

"You want me to do what?" I ask, confused about what Jodi, the pixie-looking Alpha, is proposing for my first task. I help her throw our milk cups into a garbage bag.

"You're going to be my running partner," Jodi says, nearly bursting with excitement. My stomach flips at the mere thought of my body moving at a more accelerated speed than walking. This could be very hazardous to my health, and Jodi's.

"Jodi, there's something you should know about me," I mumble, not sure how to impress upon her the gravity of this situation. "I was actually assigned to the equipment room in my high school physical education class. My teachers didn't want me anywhere near a team sport. I'm terminally klutzy."

"You're supposed to do whatever I want," she pouts.

She's right. I'm only on my first letter and I'm already trying to make excuses. If I really want to be an Alpha, I'm going to have to step out of my comfort zone. What's that saying? "Think outside of the box." My personal mantra needs to be "think outside the geek." How hard can running actually be? I nod confidently, mentally lacing up my sneakers. Jodi beams from ear to ear.

"Meet me at the track at seven," she whispers, disappearing with the bag of trash.

Wow. My first task. I was picturing some horrible hazing involving alcohol, and quite possibly animals. I always have been a little imaginative. I should have been more trusting of Lindsay when she said they would never ask us to humiliate ourselves.

"I need the pledges in the foyer please," I hear Lindsay call.

I walk around the corner, meeting Jentry and Sloane coming from the other direction. The three of us cluster around Lindsay timidly, not sure what to expect.

"I don't want you girls to think we're being rude, but you aren't allowed to stay for the second half of the meeting," Lindsay says.

"How come?" Sloane asks. I can't stand her but I'm still glad she asked.

"Let's just say that even nice girls have secrets," Lindsay

teases. "Don't worry. As soon as you are all initiated, you'll be privy to everything that goes on in the house."

The three of us nod and step out the front door.

"See you tonight, Grace Kelly," Sloane says, her voice bathed in honey. I smile and wave, acting like I don't know she is being facetious. I don't get why she's even here. I can't imagine that she would voluntarily want to spend time with such nice girls. I just hope our differences don't become a problem in the house. And I really hope she is done trying to find ways to sabotage me. I refuse to let myself think how disastrous it would be if Sloane somehow found out the truth about Edwina Fay.

· · ·

I wait for Jodi at the track that evening. I had to stop and ask for directions twice. I can't believe how turned around I get on campus without Jentry.

"Were you followed?" Jodi asks, appearing suddenly from behind a lamppost and causing me to nearly scream.

"Not that I'm aware of," I say, sweeping my glance side to side for potential stalkers.

"Okay, come over here in the grass and do some warm-ups with me." Jodi is wearing a sports bra, teeny biker shorts, and some very intense-looking tennis shoes with more gadgets on them than my watch. I feel very overdressed in my sweatshirt and sweatpants, but it's chilly out. Besides, I could never muster up the courage to walk around in just a sports bra. She stands on one foot while bending her other leg back toward her butt and grabbing it with her hand. She makes it look easy so I give it a try.

Not only does my leg not bend back the way it's supposed to, but I lose my balance and land chest first in the grass.

"Grace Kelly, quit messing around. I have to keep myself in tiptop condition. I ate two donuts this morning and they went straight to my thighs," she says, smacking her left thigh.

"Your thighs are awesome," I say, struggling to my feet. "Wait, that came out wrong."

"I used to be really fat," she says, nearly causing me to fall over again.

"Oh." I have no idea how to respond to Jodi's confession.

"The Alphas didn't care. They pledged me anyway. Being an Alpha changed my life," she admits. While I'm flattered that she feels like she can trust me with such private information, I hate that I can't think of an appropriate response.

"You look amazing now." It's the best I can do.

"Thanks. It's just something I have to battle every day," she says. "But now I'm addicted to exercise instead of food."

"I think it's really brave of you to tell me that." I feel sort of guilty about not fessing up about my recent makeover. I'm not necessarily embarrassed about who I was before my transformation. I mean, I'm still me, but I'm not planning to go around making copies of my senior picture and hanging them on all the trees on campus either.

"Someday you'll feel close enough to the sisters to tell them your secrets. That's what sisterhood is all about." She grabs me up in a quick hug, then bolts down to the track. I'm starting to see that when it comes to running, she's all business. I follow her, immediately sliding on the cinders. I take a moment to say a silent prayer for my epidermis.

Jodi removes a stopwatch from somewhere in her teeny-tiny workout outfit and starts punching some buttons on it.

"Okay, I need to run a five-minute mile. I need you to run behind me and shout out my time so I know when to start kicking it in. I don't expect you to keep up but try not to fall too far behind or I won't be able to hear you," she says, handing me the stopwatch. I look up at the well-lit track and breathe a sigh of relief. I can easily jog this entire track in five minutes, no sweat. Jodi must be kind of a slow runner if it takes her five minutes to run all the way around, but hey, what do I know?

Jodi grabs a quick drink from her water bottle, then does some more stretching and deep breathing. I'm starting to think she's a tad melodramatic.

"Are you ready?" I ask, eager to start the stopwatch and get this over with. Jodi bends down, cocks her butt in the air, and places her hands on the cinders. She's got such an intense look on her face that I almost laugh. I shouldn't be so critical. I probably look like that when I'm breaking down a chemical reaction.

"Go," she yells, jolting me back to reality. She springs into the air like a gazelle. Thankfully I remember to push the stopwatch before I start jogging, carefully, so that I don't fall too far behind her.

Before I know it, we're rounding the first bend, practically neck and neck. I start to wonder if I should fall back so I don't make her feel bad since she's the runner and all. But she wanted me to be her partner. I choose my footfalls very carefully, knowing Jentry will not be happy if I come home with a face full of cinders. I can't believe it, but I'm actually enjoying myself. We fly by the empty bleachers and I imagine masses of people screaming my name.

"What's my time?" she yells, not the least bit out of breath.

"One minute, ten seconds," I answer, a bit winded. Jodi is going to blow her time away, I think, as we approach the start of the track.

"Kicking it in now," she says, blasting ahead of me before I know what hit me. She plows right past where we started and keeps running full speed. What in the world is in those shoes of hers? I pump my arms and make myself move faster, even though my feet feel very uncomfortable at these speeds. I watch Jodi move faster and faster around the track until she eventually laps me, her feet practically smoking.

Okay, so I'm supposed to be a genius and I just figured out that obviously one time around the track isn't a mile. I try to unfold the track in a straight line in my mind to get a good idea how many times I'm going to have to lap it before this is over. I'm concentrating way too hard on measurements and not nearly enough on coordination.

My foot slips and I take a dive onto the track. It hurts, really bad.

"Are you okay?" Jodi screams from the other side of the track.

"I think so," I answer, brushing off my sweat suit. Thankfully I wasn't dressed like Jodi or I'd be picking cinders out of my skin for weeks. Luckily my face survived, but the palms of my hands weren't so lucky. "Three minutes, forty seconds," I yell as Jodi sprints past me. I doubt Jodi is going to mind if I hang up my tennis shoes, so I wobble back over to the grass and squat down.

I get sort of bummed, knowing I didn't accomplish my task. Why do I have to be so uncoordinated? It's like my body parts and brain can't communicate with each other. I pull a clump of grass and toss it away in frustration.

Jodi sails up, barely out of breath. I hit the button on the stopwatch. "Wow, five minutes, forty-two seconds. You were awesome," I tell her.

She collapses next to me in the grass.

"You better do some more of those stretching exercises. You don't want your lactic acid building up," I tell her, pulling random knowledge from some orifice.

She looks at me and giggles. "What are you talking about?"

I'm about to break into a full spiel on the three systems that produce energy to resynthesize Adenosine Triphosphate, but somehow I don't think Jodi will appreciate the beauty of the formula. "Just do some cool downs or your muscles will be really sore," I tell her.

She nods and starts stretching in poses that I didn't know were physically possible. Just one day I'd like to be at peace with my body, I think, picking more cinders out of the knees of my sweat suit.

"You're so lucky," Jodi says, gazing over at me.

"Huh?" I ask, confused. Is she being sarcastic or what?

"Being so smart. I'd love to be as smart as you are," she says, jumping up.

"If I'm so smart, why can't I manage to get my feet to do what I want?" I ask, disgusted.

"We can't all be good at the same thing or it would be a pretty boring world, Grace Kelly," she laughs, pulling me up.

She's absolutely right. Okay, so maybe I'm not the most graceful person on the face of the earth, but I'm definitely smart. Who cares if I can't run a mile under six minutes? I'm a rock star with a Bunsen burner.

"So, did I complete my first task?" I ask, excited.

"One down, twenty-five to go," Jodi confirms.

I'm starting to think that these tasks are going to be a really good thing. I get to spend individual time with most of the sisters while proving my loyalty to them. Besides, I've always worked for anything else I wanted. Why should the Alphas be any different? Once my twenty-sixth task is complete, I'll know that I've earned my spot with the Alphas, even if I lied to get here.

• • •

The Alpha house is alive with lights and music as Jodi and I approach it.

"The Welcome Back Mixer. I totally forgot," I say, disappointed. "I'm never going to have time to get back to the dorm, get ready, then get back here before the Omegas leave," I say, depressed. I can't believe I forgot. I've been looking forward to this all day. When I found out the Alphas were hosting Charlie's fraternity, the Omega Tau Nus, I almost burst with excitement at the thought of seeing him. But in my sweat-stained workout clothes and dorky headband, I look way too much like the old me to risk seeing him like this, even if I was probably wearing something very similar at the science fair last spring.

"You can wear something of mine," Jodi offers. We tiptoe through the door, neither of us wanting to be questioned about the task. The door leads into the kitchen and we take the back staircase to Jodi's second-floor bedroom.

"Pick whatever you want," she says, stripping down faster than I knew was humanly possible and disappearing into her bathroom.

Laughter curls up through the registers from downstairs. I throw off my sweatshirt in anticipation of a few laughs with Charlie tonight, and hopefully some more flirting that maybe I'll actually be able to pick up on. I can hardly wait to point Charlie out to Jentry. I throw open Jodi's closet and flip on the light. I'm pleasantly surprised when I realize that all of her clothes are hung up by color families. Jodi has even stuck to the ROY G. BIV mnemonic in the placement sequence of hues. If I had more time, I would help even further by arranging them from long sleeve to short sleeve, representing the decrease in wavelength, making her closet the perfect visible spectrum. I can't believe I didn't think to sort my closet this way!

It doesn't take long to realize that my boobs are way bigger than Jodi's. Button-down shirts are definitely out. I groan while flipping through all of her extra-small T-shirts. I have a choice to make. I either show up to the mixer in my stinky, sweaty shirt that I wore to the track, or I show up squeezed into one of Jodi's tees, looking like a wet T-shirt contestant. I yank a black tee with rhinestones that spell out "high maintenance" and pull it over my head. I peel off my sweatpants and slide into a pair of old jeans that fit perfectly.

"Wow, you look great," Jodi says, coming up behind me wrapped in a towel.

"Really?" I ask, surveying myself in her full-length mirror.

"Total hottie. My makeup and hair stuff is over there. Help yourself." She points to a vanity before going into her walk-in closet to get dressed.

I use a face wipe to clean off my sweaty pores, then very carefully apply some of Jodi's makeup. I twist a few curls into my still-damp hair and spray it so it doesn't frizz the minute I walk out of the room. I dab on some lip gloss and give myself another once-over. I'm still not used to my reflection in the mirror. If I didn't know better, I'd think the girl staring back at me really was high maintenance. I practice a few smiles so I don't look like a total dork when I see Charlie.

"The Omegas are gonna be all over you, girl," Jodi laughs, emerging from her closet in a hot-pink silk tank top and mini-skirt. She fixes her hair and makeup and soon we're descending the stairs to the party.

"I'm nervous," I admit, fidgeting with my pledge pin on the collar of my shirt.

"You did really great today, Grace Kelly. Listen to your heart and you'll find your place here," she says cryptically. She gets swallowed up by a group of Greeks and is gone before I can ask her what she means.

"There you are," Jentry shouts, grabbing my arm.

"I would tell you where I've been, but then I'd have to kill you," I joke. She looks adorable in a white shirtdress with cranberry-colored tights poking out from underneath. Jentry could make a garbage bag look good.

"Love the shirt," she says, winking at me. "This is Ron," she says, introducing me to the extremely muscular Omega that she was deep in conversation with before seeing me.

"Nice to meet you. I'm Grace Kelly or GK," I say, holding my hand out. His face lights up as he nearly pumps my hand off my body.

"I know who you are. You're the chick who gave Miller the lump on his head." He starts laughing uncontrollably.

"Guilty," I admit, not sure if it is a good thing that Charlie told him about me or not.

Before I can obsess over it, I feel someone pulling on my arm. I turn to see Brock, an active, looking frantic.

"What's wrong, Brock?" I ask, concerned.

"Kelly needs to see you in the bathroom right away."
She rushes off before I can ask why a sister would possibly
want me to meet her in the bathroom. This gives a whole
new meaning to being close.

"I guess I've gotta go. We'll catch up later," I tell Jentry.
She nods, having already gone back to ogling her muscular
Omega man.

I rush to the half bath near the staircase and knock
lightly on the door. A delicate arm reaches out and pulls
me into the bathroom.

"Kelly, what's wrong?" I say, taking in her teased hair,
shorter-than-short jean shorts, and bikini top.

"I need to give you your task. Now listen. I know we
are supposed to be picking stuff that builds your character and all that crap, but there's something that the Alphas
need to do to keep a good reputation with the Omegas.
They're starting to think that we're all a bunch of goody-
goodies." She turns up her nose in disgust. "*B* is for beer.
The Omegas brought their beer bong and none of the
other girls will try it. The guys are getting bored just standing around drinking. We've got to liven up this mixer or
the guys are going to bail and head to the Zeta house." She
sucks her breath in at the mere thought that the Omegas
would ditch the Alphas for the skanky Zetas.

I blow out a huge sigh of relief. I don't exactly know
what a beer bong is, but I know it's gotta be better than the
B task I was imagining. Besides, I don't want Charlie bail-
ing on the mixer before I even get a chance to talk to him.

"Sure, I'll do it," I agree. Kelly jumps up and down,

knocking my hip into the corner of the bathroom counter. Pants were definitely a good choice tonight, to hide all my battle scars.

• • •

Five minutes later, I'm again thankful I wore jeans. As if drinking beer sitting right side up wasn't bad enough, I'm now inverted with a plastic PVC pipe stuck between my lips, trying not to gag as the urine-smelling beer flows into my mouth. I pretend it's Mountain Dew and chug as fast as I can. I try not to think about Charlie's hands around my ankles holding me in the air. I try to tune out all the people chanting my name. I *do* calculate, based on my height and weight, how much beer I would have to drink to get smashed. I quickly realize that I passed that amount about three gulps ago.

After what feels like an eternity, someone removes the tube from my mouth and several hands are on my back and arms spinning me right side up again. Everyone is clapping and screaming, but I'm too dizzy to care. Charlie steadies me by grabbing my shoulders. He is laughing and saying something about how cool I am. If he only knew. He leans in, his eyes on my lips. Is he really going to kiss me right here in front of everybody?

My eyes dart behind him to Jentry, who gives me a thumbs-up. I look back to Charlie, whose lips are clos-ing in on me at an alarming speed. My stomach gurgles in panic. Charlie closes his eyes and his lips are so close to mine that I can feel his breath. I close my eyes and pray that I know what I'm doing. I lick my lips and take a deep breath. To my horror, the breath comes back out as the biggest burp I've ever let out, right in Charlie's face.

SIX

"I swallowed some air when I was upside-down and then when it combined with the air that was already in my stomach from the bacteria that forms gases—"

"It's cool, Grace Kelly. If you didn't want to kiss me, you should have just told me," Charlie says, cutting off the detailed explanation I was about to give for why I burped in his face.

"But I *did* want to kiss you," I say, realizing too late that I put way too much emphasis on the word did.

It took a few minutes for the roar of laughter after my burp to die down, but once it did, it was like everyone realized Charlie and I needed to be alone. So here we are, tucked in a corner of the kitchen. Alone.

"So maybe I should try again," Charlie says, leaning toward me.

This is it. My very first kiss. What if I screw it up?

What if I open my mouth too far or not enough? What if I have beer burp breath? What if…

"Are you in pain?" Charlie asks, looking concerned. I realize that by trying to focus on not screwing up the kiss I probably look like I'm constipated. I'm sure that's an attractive face. Now Charlie will never want to kiss me.

My first thought after realizing Charlie is already kissing me is that I don't ever want him to stop. His lips are like delicious plump pillows of skin. Okay, that didn't come out right, but I can't believe how good this feels. Charlie wraps his arms around me to pull me closer to him. I mimic his gesture while trying not to overthink what my lips seem to automatically know how to do. I do make a mental note to Google how many nerve endings lips have. Charlie seems to know how to hit every single one.

"Oh, crap. Sorry, Grace Kelly, but I really need to see you in the other room," I hear a sister saying from behind me at the same time my cell phone vibrates in my pocket. I jerk away from Charlie like I'm being electrocuted. It's amazing the power my mother has over me, even from miles away.

"It's okay, Susie. Um, bye," I mumble to Charlie, disappearing out of the kitchen behind Susie. I'm so embarrassed I can't even look at him.

As we make our way through the house, I realize I'm not the only one whose lips were getting a workout. Jentry and her muscle man are stashed away in a corner of the foyer when Susie and I jog up the steps to the bedrooms. Jentry opens an eye and winks at me, then grabs the guy's butt. I stifle a laugh, sensing Susie's serious demeanor.

"The girls are in my room," Susie says, leading me into a bedroom that looks as if a cotton candy machine exploded in it. Two other sisters, Brittney and Juliet, are waiting cross-legged on the bed. Susie shuts the door and joins them. I stay standing, knowing I'm about to get my third task. By this rate, I'll be on *Z* before next weekend.

"Are you aware of the rivalry between Alpha Alpha Alpha and Zeta Sigma Alpha?" Brittney asks, her innocent features clouding up with hatred.

"Not really," I admit, wondering if there was some dossier of Alpha rivals I should have read up on.

"Those girls are poison. They've stolen our boyfriends, started vicious rumors about us, and worst of all, dominated the university cheerleading squad for years. Alphas aren't even allowed to try out. It's a travesty and we're sick of it," Juliet shouts, shaking her head in disgust. Brittney moves over to touch her arm, which seems to calm Juliet down a bit.

"We've been presented with the perfect opportunity for a little payback at the football game tomorrow. And that's where you come in," Susie explains.

"Um, okay," I respond nervously.

"The mascot is going to be down with food poisoning tomorrow and you are going to borrow her uniform to sneak into the girl's locker room. Once you get in, you need to go through all the lockers and take out their cheer panties. Then you'll use this," Susie says, waving a large box cutter at me. "You are going to slice a line through the back of their panties, right down the middle. When they bend over for their big half-time show, they'll flash their butts to the entire crowd and get thrown off the squad." The three of them squeal with joy at the thought of the entire cheerleading squad mooning some poor spectators.

"How do you know the school mascot is going to get sick?" I ask.

Brittney fans her face with a stack of dollar bills and I suddenly get it.

"What if I get in trouble?" I ask, hating that I sound so paranoid. Grace Kelly was the scaredy-cat always playing by the rules; GK should never be asking such a goody-goody question. But she is, or I mean, I am.

"You'll be wearing the mascot uniform, so nobody will know it's you. If you get caught in the locker room, just run. But you'll be in there really early so no one else will be there," Suzie says.

I hate to be so paranoid, but I've never been in any trouble my entire life. Not so much as an overdue library book. Now I'm expected to hijack the school's mascot and slash a bunch of panties?

"It will count for *C*, *P*, and *Z*," Brittney adds. As much as it drives me crazy that my tasks obviously aren't going to continue in a sequential order, I agree.

"How do I get the uniform?" I ask. Susie tosses something from behind the bed. A huge bundle hits me square in the chest. It's a zippered bag that formal gowns are normally kept in. I unzip it to find a polyester-blend nightmare of black and white. I don't know how it slipped my mind that our school mascot is a zebra. As much as I love McMillan College's mission statement ("It doesn't matter how you look at the world, just as long as you do"), and how the whole "is a zebra white with black stripes or black with white stripes?" fits in with that, I still don't particularly want to dress up like one.

"Here's the head," Susie says, tossing a purple suitcase at me. The four of us die laughing as I pop it on my head and start prancing around the room. Maybe this won't be so bad after all, maybe it will actually be fun, or maybe I'm still buzzing from drinking all that beer.

• • •

A few minutes later I'm back downstairs trying to find a closet that I can stash my obnoxious zebra pelt in. The party is still in full swing. It looks like my beer bonging paid off. I skulk around the edges of different groups trying not to be too obvious while I look for Charlie. I don't know why, but I'm actually kind of relieved when I can't find him. The kiss was delish but my cheeks are burning just at the thought of facing him. My phone vibrates angrily in my pocket again and I quickly bolt out the front door to answer it. If Mom heard bump-and-grind music in the background, she would be here in a couple of hours to pack up my stuff and take me back home.

"Hi, Mom," I say, praying there isn't some new technology that enables the person calling to smell your breath. Mom's voice is the vocal equivalent of black coffee.

"You sound different, Grace," Mom says. I don't miss the edge in her voice.

"I think I might be coming down with something," I fudge, immediately hating myself for needlessly worrying her.

"Meningitis spreads like wildfire on college campuses. You should get to health services immediately," she demands.

"Mom, it's not meningitis. I'm fine, I promise."

"Prove it. Take a picture of yourself and send it to me."

"Right now?" I glance around at the tall columns next to me, and the row of fraternity and sorority houses to my left and right. Not a good photo op. My only other option is to stand out in the darkened quad. Not to mention that my own mother wouldn't even recognize me since my makeover. I'm not sure which would give her a heart attack faster, the makeover or the fact that I'm rushing a sorority.

"The camera on my phone is busted, Mom. I dropped it yesterday," I say, doing some quick thinking.

I hear a small hiccup on the line and I'm positive she's crying. The whole empty nest thing is definitely not a myth. I suddenly feel extremely guilty for lying to her. I wish I could tell her the truth. That I've found an incredible group of girls that like me, and for once, I might actually fit in somewhere. Of course, I'd leave out the part about all the panties I have to slash tomorrow. And the beer bong. And the boy I kissed. But to be honest, I'm a little overwhelmed by all of these new experiences. It would be nice to have her opinion. But if I told her everything I've done, she would never trust me enough to let me stay. And there is no way I'm leaving college.

"Excuse me, miss," a man says, tapping me on the shoulder. I jerk my head up, startled. Two campus police guards are standing in front of me, looking very serious.

"Um, Mom, I'm getting pretty tired. I'll call you tomorrow," I say, clicking off.

Even though this is my first official kegger, I'm smart enough to know it isn't a good thing when the campus police show up. The Alphas aren't even being rowdy. I wonder how they knew we were having a party?

"Have you been drinking tonight, miss?" one of the officers asks me. I go to stand up from the step to face him when I slip and nearly sprain my ankle. "That's it. Let me see some identification," he says, convinced I'm hammered.

"No, you don't understand. I'm just normally klutzy," I say, dialing Jentry's cell phone number behind my back. I have to try and give the sisters a heads-up. I just hope she isn't too busy making out with that muscle-head to hear her phone ringing.

"So are you saying you haven't been drinking tonight?" the other cop asks, glaring at me hatefully.

"I don't drink," I answer, which was true up until about an hour ago.

"Then you won't mind agreeing to a sobriety test, will you?" they both say in unison.

I shrug my shoulders, knowing that I don't really have

a choice. Between the beer and my natural klutziness, this is going to go down really bad.

"Repeat the alphabet. Backwards," one of them says, looking smug.

I try hard not to smile as I easily repeat the alphabet backwards with record speed. I almost feel bad for the security guards as they stand with their mouths wide open after I say "*A*." How could they have possibly known how much time I spent in the great room today gazing at the giant letters hanging on the wall that hold my fate?

• • •

"You totally saved us," Lindsay says, gathering up plastic cups and other trash while I hold open the garbage bag for her.

I smile nervously. It's been an hour since my run-in with the security guards and I'm still not quite back to normal. When I started to think about how much trouble I could have gotten into, I nearly hyperventilated. And I don't even want to think about what would happen if Mom found out.

"My hero," Jentry swoons, resting her head on my shoulder. I think she is still buzzing, not from beer but from Ron. All the other sisters agree with Jentry and are beaming at me as we clean up the house.

"It was nothing," I say, loving the extra attention. I bet Sloane is nearly foaming at the mouth with jealousy. I look around the room, but surprisingly, I don't see her demon eyes glaring back at me. "Where's Sloane?" I ask, disappointed that she is missing out on the sisters fawning over me.

"She went home sick earlier. The poor thing was absolutely green," Lindsay confirms.

What horrible timing, I think, and then proceed to forget all about Sloane and bask in the glow of my sisters' adoration.

SEVEN

The next morning I wake up from a dream about Charlie. I squeeze my eyes tight in hopes of getting back to it when I hear one of the snaps on the suitcase that Brittney and Juliet gave me last night click open. I bolt up in bed.

"Don't. I'm serious," I yell. Jentry looks up, probably surprised that I can be forceful when I want to.

"What have you got stashed in here? Like a head or something?" she giggles, but backs away from the offending suitcase.

"Let's just say that I don't want you to be an accomplice and leave it at that," I tell her, trying not to laugh at how right on she is about a head being in the suitcase. I'm so nervous that I'm going to get busted today. I wonder what exactly my punishment would be for dressing up like a monochromatic mammal that sneaks into locker rooms and violates cheerleaders' panties? I'm pretty sure I don't want to know.

"The sisters were seriously impressed with you last night," Jentry says, referring to the secretive phone call I made while dazzling the campus police with my reverse alphabetical knowledge.

"I'm just glad the Omegas were able to sneak the keg back to their house so the Alphas didn't get in trouble." I'd be lying if I didn't confess to how cool it was when the girls found out that I saved the house from getting in big trouble.

"I wonder who called security?" Jentry asks, making her bed.

"Maybe they were just walking around and heard the party." Even though I loved the extra attention I got last night, I was glad when Lindsay announced that there would be no more alcohol in the Alpha house because it was too risky.

"I'm guessing you have a busy day?" Jentry asks, turning on her cell phone. It beeps that she has a message and a huge smile breaks over her sleepy face as she listens to it.

"Let me guess? Ron?" I tease her.

"He just can't get enough of me," she laughs. I start to remind her of her guy strike but then I realize I wasn't exactly picketing boys last night when I was kissing Charlie.

My face starts getting hot and prickly just thinking about his arms around me. Besides the whole burping-in-his-face incident, I couldn't have had a more perfect first kiss. Or kisses.

"So, you and Charlie seemed to be examining the heck out of each other's tonsils," Jentry teases.

"For some reason, I think he really likes me," I admit, amazed. The makeover and the bid from the Alphas has done wonders for my self-esteem, but sometimes I feel my old issues rising back up again. "I mean, there is the whole debate about pheromones and all ... " I trail off, still unable to fully grasp how a boy as cute and funny as Charlie is giving me the time of day.

"Build a bridge, GK. You're a hottie Alpha pledge now. Charlie would be lucky to scrape the gum off your shoes for you," she laughs.

She's right. Why wouldn't Charlie like me? I'm smart, funny, and nice, and while I'm not quite sure about the hottie part, I know I feel a lot more confident about my appearance than I ever have before. Grace Kelly was the one with the self-esteem issues, not GK. It's time to start thinking like GK all the time.

"I'm outta here," I say, jumping up and into a pair of khaki shorts and an Alpha tank top. I wrap my hair in a ponytail since it is just going to be crammed in the zebra head anyway.

"We both got *A* and *B* yesterday. You'll be done with this Alpha Bet in no time," she says confidently. I wish I could ask about her tasks, but I respect the sisterly bonding that the tasks are meant to promote too much to jeopardize it by asking her.

"We'll catch up later?" I ask, pausing at the open door with my suitcase and formal dress bag in my arms.

"Sure. You know, if you're back from the prom in time."
I stick my tongue out at her and pull the door closed. Prom.
I wish.

• • •

"Are you sure no one is here?" I ask, paranoid that some of
the other sisters might still be in the Alpha house.

"For the third time, no one is here," Susie informs me.
She flings open her bedroom door as proof.

"This thing is really hot," I complain as Susie, Brittney,
and Juliet zip up the back of the zebra costume. I wonder
if they could make a deal with the sister who has *W* and
I could get credit for that one too because of the weight
loss I'm going to have traipsing around in this costume in
ninety-degree heat. I'll be lucky if I don't pass out, and I
don't even have the head on yet.

"Stop complaining. You look cute," Juliet laughs.

"Totally," Brittney adds, fluffing up my fur.

"It's not every girl who can pull off stripes," Susie pipes
up.

"Thanks," I say, trying to be a good sport and not waste
any excess energy that I have a feeling I'm going to need
later.

"We really appreciate this, Grace Kelly. This isn't just
some petty prank. The Zetas are truly evil," Brittney clarifies.

"We've tried to rise above it but they just won't leave us
alone," Juliet says, pounding her fist into her palm.

"Calm down, Juliet. We don't know for sure they're the ones who tried to get us busted last night," Susie says, running a hairbrush over my costume.

"Are you kidding me? They would do anything to get our charter revoked," Juliet yells.

"You know what they say about paybacks," Brittney laughs. While I completely get the whole sorority rival thing, I'm pretty sure I'm well on my way to heat stroke. I stumble toward the door, hoping this goes quickly.

"Do you know where to go?" Susie asks, plopping down on the bed.

"The McMurray Athletic Building, girl's locker room," I confirm.

"Perfect. Just think, Grace Kelly, in twenty minutes, you'll be three letters closer to becoming a full-blown Alpha," Juliet adds, giving me a wink.

Or I'll be in the custody of campus security.

• • •

Surprisingly, finding my way to the athletic building through two tiny eyeholes wasn't hard at all. Getting into the girls' locker room isn't nearly as easy. Susie, Brittney, and Juliet failed to mention that there would be football players straggling around in the hallways. I know they don't know who I am but it freaks me out that several people witnessed me going into the locker room. Granted, they couldn't exactly pick me out of a lineup unless I was wearing this costume, but I still feel like I could puke. Mom would die if she saw what I was up to.

I stumble down the corridor and pull open the door to the girls' locker room. I expect to see a room full of cheerleaders with their fangs and claws drawn, just waiting for me. My blood pressure is way over the recommended 120/80 guidelines right now. But all I see are half-opened gray lockers with cheer skirts and pom-poms cascading out of them.

I don't even give myself time to think about backing out of this. I grab the box cutter from my hidden pocket and start rifling through lockers for panties. This feels wrong on so many levels. But as I slice through the back of the first pair of cheer panties, I get sort of giddy. It is kind of fun to be bad. I never got to TP or egg anyone's house on Halloween like the kids I went to school with. I always had to go to the fire station for donuts and chocolate milk with my parents and Sean.

My curfew was seven o'clock. Not like I had anyone trying to make hot plans with me or anything, but even if someone had tried, Mom's mandatory curfew would have made it impossible to have a life. I slice through the second pair of panties with a vengeance, my temper flaring when I think about how Mom's paranoia stunted my emotional growth and maturity.

When all the other girls my age were getting their first bra, I begged my mom to buy me one that I spotted at the mall. She blew me off. I attempted to make my own out of shoestrings and gauze pads, but it didn't quite hold up. She never wanted me to grow up.

I was furious just remembering how I felt that day. Before I even realize what I'm doing, I have a pile of cut-up cheer panties sitting on the metal bench outside of the lockers. They are covered with tufts of black and white fur and I realize that in my fury I've accidentally cut off parts of my fake fur. Oops. Thinking about Mom's over protectiveness makes me crazy.

I get to work stuffing the panties back into the lockers. I'm hoping they are one size fits all because I don't remember which ones go where. I'm just putting the last pair back when I hear the door open and several high-pitched voices coming toward me.

I start to panic trying to figure out how to get out unseen. The only place to hide is some empty lockers but there is no way I can fit inside one of them with this costume on.

"What the hell are you doing in here?" a vicious-looking brunette says as she rounds the corner. Four more similar-looking girls appear behind her back. All of them are eyeing me as I imagine a hungry lion would in the Serengeti.

"I got lost," I say, holding my hooves out to my sides, hoping I look confused.

"You're so pathetic. How many times do I have to tell you that we aren't going to let you on the squad?"

I try to sidestep the brunette, hoping I can just make a run for it. Her cronies block my view of the exit and glare menacingly into my eyeholes. I have a feeling this is going to turn out very badly.

"Get her, girls," the brunette demands. The female pride of cheerleaders surrounds me like I'm the weakest in the herd. This is worth way more than three letters. In a swift move that I wouldn't have thought myself capable of on a good day, let alone wearing a giant smelly zebra head, I pounce onto the metal bench towering a good foot above them. I know I can't jump high enough to clear them so I decide to take a more direct approach.

I dive at the two closest to the exit, taking them by surprise. As I fly through the air, I think my sneak attack is brilliant. But then I remember Sir Isaac Newton's Laws of Gravitation and that what goes up, must come down. I hear the thud but am pleasantly surprised not to feel much pain. I don't think the two girls I landed on can say the same. They are writhing around, moaning. I scramble to my hooves and bolt out of the locker room.

"Get back here, you crazy pachyderm," one of the girls yells.

It takes everything I have not to turn around and correct her. Doesn't she know that calling a zebra an elephant is the equivalent of saying humans were alive during the Jurassic Era? Maybe the cheerleader stereotype isn't that far off after all.

I fly out of the locker room only to run smack into someone. All I see is blonde hair go tumbling down. I keep running, afraid that the cheerleaders are close on my hooves. I feel guilty about not helping my casualty up though.

"Jesus, kill me why don't you?" I hear the blonde scream down the hall. I stop and turn around to see Sloane brushing herself off. What in the world is she doing here? Then I remember that she has tasks, too. The Alphas must have more in store for the Zetas. I'm just glad my tasks are over. And not only did I just get three more letters but I got to knock Sloane on her butt as a bonus.

I bust through the doors and out into the bright September afternoon. I'm immediately broiling and I have to find a place to get this head off before my body temperature rises to a dangerous level. I can already feel my thirst mechanism kicking in and I would guess that I've already sweat out close to a pound of water. It is critical that I get my hands on something with electrolytes in it, pronto.

I'm getting a bit dizzy so I disappear behind a few large oaks on campus. I strip off the costume and shove it into a large plastic bag I stuck in the pocket of my shorts. I immediately feel better, but I still need something to drink. I figure Susie, Brittney, and Juliet will be glued to the campus television channel that is broadcasting the football game. They'll see I completed my tasks so I don't need to hurry back to the Alpha house.

The campus is mostly deserted as I head into the student center. I stash the costume behind an overstuffed couch in a corner. I scan my student ID to pay for a lemon-lime Gatorade, unscrew the top, and don't stop guzzling until I've ingested the entire twenty ounces.

"Remind me to never challenge you to a drink-off," Charlie's voice says from behind me.

I spin around, dribbling the last few drops of Gatorade on my pink tank. I try to quickly brush them off but they have already penetrated the material. My stain stick has been getting a workout lately.

"Oh, I just came from a run," I say, trying to sound convincing, knowing my hair must be a mess after being stuck in that head.

"You should come sit down. Your face is pretty red," he says, looking worried.

"It was kind of an intense workout," I say, not completely lying. A bunch of deranged cheerleaders chasing you would get anybody's heart rate up. I move over to the couch and sink into the cushions. Charlie sits down on the section next to me.

"I thought everybody was at the football game," he says.

"I'm not much of a sports fan," I admit, noticing a flat screen televising the game behind Charlie's head.

"Yeah, me neither," he agrees. "Are you looking forward to classes starting on Monday?"

"Actually, I am." It's been nice to have time to acclimate to college life and meet new people, but I'm ready to flip open a new notebook and fill it with exciting knowledge. Learning is my comfort zone and after this crazy week, I'm ready to get back to it.

"Is it completely nerdy to admit that I look forward to seeing the class syllabus for the first time?" Charlie laughs, hiding his face with his hands.

"Me, too," I agree wholeheartedly.

We chat easily for a few minutes until I notice the

cheerleaders gallop onto the field for the half-time show. The sound is muted but I can tell the music has started by their synchronized movements.

"Good game, huh?" Charlie asks, turning around to see the television. Right then the cheerleaders spin around and bend over, giving their viewing audience a little more than they expected. The channel immediately cuts to a commercial.

"That's something you don't see every day," Charlie snorts.

I can't control the huge grin that breaks across my face, knowing how pleased the Alphas are going to be.

• • •

Later at the house, the sisters are all abuzz about the Zetas. Most of them have figured out that the Alphas were behind it even though the task has never been mentioned.

"That was the most awesome thing I have ever seen," Juliet gushes.

"Cheerleaders, panties, zebra," Brittney chants as she tears down the *C*, *P*, and *Z* papers from the great room walls. I love watching those papers come down. We leave the great room and wander into the kitchen.

The rest of the sisters are crowded in the kitchen fixing snacks and giggling excitedly about the Zeta prank. The active sisters can't openly praise me because of the secrecy of the tasks, but several of them have patted me on the back, squeezed my arm, or given me a thumbs-up sign.

Jentry winks at me over her turkey sandwich but looks exhausted. I search around for Sloane, feeling a tad guilty about plowing into her, but I don't see her.

"Where's Sloane?" I ask.

"Oh, the poor thing ended up having the stomach flu. She's been holed up in her dorm room since last night," Lindsay says sympathetically.

I'm about to raise my eyebrows at Jentry to tip her off that Sloane lied to the sisters when I realize this could be part of a task. Maybe Lindsay is lying to us so that Sloane can complete a task. I would look like a tattle tail if I said something about seeing Sloane today. I grab a chip and stuff it in my mouth instead. Besides, I'm looking forward to a nice, drama-free evening with the sisters.

My cell phone vibrates in my pocket. I pull it out to see a text message from Sean. Something tells me it is going to be a comment about the cheerleaders. Dad and Sean never miss a McMillan game. His message reads: 911. Mom on way.

I drop my cell phone on the ceramic tile and I'm pretty sure I don't have to lie about the camera not working anymore.

EIGHT

"She's trying to ruin my life," I whine to Dad. Thankfully I caught him on his cell phone before they could leave.

"I know she's a tad bit overbearing sometimes Grace, but you are only sixteen," Dad reminds me, as if I need reminding that I have this huge underage secret hanging over me. "She just wants to make sure that you are exactly the way she left you."

That's the problem. I'm nothing like the way she left me. Just a week ago, I wouldn't have dreamed of bonding with the most popular girls on campus. Today, they're my sisters.

"Even Sean misses you," Dad says, interrupting my thoughts.

"Now I know you're full of it," I laugh.

"Seriously Grace, it's not the same around here without

you. I guess instead of you being homesick, the rest of us are homesick for you."

Okay, so I was a bit nostalgic for our family game night the other night, and it would be kind of nice to see my family, if only I knew that my mom wouldn't completely freak out about my new appearance. And, of course, there is no way I can tell her about the Alphas.

"I've made some changes," I admit. I figure I'll let Dad do my dirty work and tell Mom about the enhanced version of me. That way she'll have some advance notice.

"I'm not going to want to hear this, am I?"

"I cut my hair, got contacts, and I don't wear anything with elastic anymore," I charge forward, feeling good that I am finally being honest.

"The only thing that matters is that you feel good about yourself," Dad says sweetly.

"I do, Dad. I really do."

• • •

I hang up with Dad and scour my dorm room for Alpha affiliations. I shove my Alpha tank top and a picture frame that one of the sisters made me in the bottom of one of my drawers. I'm trying to find a hiding place for a picture of Jentry and me together at the Alpha-Omega party the other night when she walks in.

"You look scary," she says, dropping her bookbag near her desk. "And way to be sneaky," she adds, grabbing the box cutter off my bed. It must have slipped out of my pocket.

Oops.

"I will have you know that I did not cut myself once today," I reply, proud of myself.

"Well, that's something."

I hide my Alpha pledge pin inside an argyle sock. This must be like the cardinal Alpha sin, but my mom isn't naïve enough to think it is just an innocent accessory.

"Nobody is going to steal your Alpha pin, GK," Jentry says, rolling her eyes.

"My parents are coming to take me out to dinner," I tell her, sitting down to do my makeup.

"Holy crap! Why aren't you totally freaking out right now?" she asks, jumping around the room.

"I already told my dad about my makeover and it's not like I'm going to volunteer that I'm pledging a sorority," I say, surprisingly calm.

"Wow," Jentry says, shaking her head. "They aren't even going to recognize you and it won't have anything to do with your hair and makeup."

"Besides ... I thought maybe you could come with us," I plead, giving her my best puppy dog eyes. I nearly stab myself in the eye with eyeliner in the process.

"Oh, hell no," she shouts.

"Please. I'll totally owe you," I plead.

"What about the Alpha sleepover?"

"We'll be back with time to spare. It's just dinner. My parents will treat," I singsong.

"Is your pervy little brother coming?" She smiles.

"You think he would miss a chance to drool over you?"

"It would be kind of fun to mess with him," she ponders. "I'm in."

"Yay! Okay, I already have it planned out. We'll go find a restaurant off campus so that we won't run into anybody. As long as neither one of us slips and mentions the sorority, or that your mom is actually alive, we'll be golden." It's the perfect plan. What could possibly go wrong?

• • •

"Dang, sis. You look smokin," Sean says, quickly moving his eyes from me to Jentry. She pinches his cheek playfully.

I hold my breath waiting for my parents' reaction. Surprisingly, my mother doesn't look like she'll be needing a paper bag to breathe in and out of. My dad is grinning like a maniac behind her so I know he approves. A tear slips down my mother's cheek and I contemplate running back to barricade myself in my dorm. What if she thinks college is having a negative impact on me and makes me come home? There is no way I would survive after my brief taste of the outside world.

"Hi, Mom," I say apprehensively.

"Grace Kelly," she says quietly. "You look gorgeous."

Huh? She grabs me up in a hug before I can fully process her approval.

"You're having a good influence on her, Jentry," Mom says, backing out of our hug but not taking her eyes off me. Jentry seems to beam from the compliment.

"I missed you guys," I say, backing out of the hug.

Until this moment, I hadn't really thought I missed anything about home, but seeing the three of them and getting their approval feels even better than it did to escape the deranged cheerleaders earlier.

We head out to the parking lot to my parents' minivan. Sean not-so-subtly scores the seat next to Jentry. He's so pathetic.

"So where do the kids go to escape the dorm food around here?" Dad jokes.

"I saw a pizza place down the street," Sean interrupts. I know that he is referring to the same pizza place Jentry and I went to my first night here. The official Greek hangout.

"Actually, Mr. Cook, there is a stir-fry place I've been wanting to try if it's okay with you and Mrs. Cook," Jentry pipes up while removing Sean's hand from her knee. Jentry and I exchange a knowing glance. It is so awesome to have someone who is watching my back.

"Point the way," Dad agrees enthusiastically. I lean back into the van seat, relieved to have dodged one bullet. Now if I can just make it through this meal without tipping my mom off that I've joined a sorority.

• • •

"Go easy on the seafood, Grace Kelly," Mom says, as I continue to pile shrimp on top of the snow peas already in my bowl. "Your grandpa developed an allergy to shellfish late in life."

"Mom, seriously," I warn. Jentry snorts into her hand behind me.

Mom continues down the buffet, sulking. Her bowl is practically empty. I guess the new me has made her lose her appetite. She makes her way to the table where Dad and Sean are already pigging out.

"She's actually handling things extremely well," Jentry says, gesturing toward Mom.

"I'm sure the best is yet to come. Eat fast," I joke. I have to admit that Mom's reaction was much better than I had anticipated. I just don't want to get my hopes up. The calm before the storm and all that.

Jentry and I head over to the table to join my parents. Sean jumps up with a noodle hanging out of his mouth and pulls out Jentry's chair. I exchange a glance with my parents and we all nearly double over with laughter at Sean's sudden chivalrous nature.

I tuck my cloth napkin into the collar of my shirt. I'm not about to take the chance of dropping something down the front of my shirt when I'm trying to show my parents my new sophisticated self.

"So, classes start on Monday, huh?" Dad asks, stabbing a baby corncob with his fork.

"Finally," I answer between huge bitefuls of shrimp. "I can't wait."

"How about you, Jentry? Are you ready?" Mom asks. I already warned Dad that talking about Jentry's dead (or not) mother was off limits tonight.

"Well, I don't have a brain like GK, um, Grace Kelly's,

so I'll have to work pretty hard to keep up," Jentry admits. I put my fork down and look over at her.

"Not with me as a roommate, you won't," I say confidently. I'm glad that I will finally be able to help Jentry after everything she has done for me. My brain is already whizzing with different study aids I could make to help Jentry with her classes.

"If anybody can help you, it's Grace Kelly. She's definitely the brains of the family," Dad chuckles.

"Yeah, no pressure being the sibling of a genius," Sean pipes up. "All of my teachers keep asking me if I'm going to graduate from high school at sixteen like my sister did. As if."

Everything seems to slow down. I watch Jentry drop her fork as it's midway to her mouth. She quickly recovers it and pretends to be extremely interested in her noodles. Leave it to Sean to open his big mouth.

"Why wouldn't you buy me a bra?" I ask Mom, partly to distract Jentry from learning the truth about my age, and partly because I really want to know.

"Grace Kelly, what on earth are you talking about?" Mom turns to Jentry and apologizes with her eyes. Jentry smiles uncomfortably and gets very interested in a forkful of rice.

"I'm talking about the day that you and I went to the mall and I wanted a bra and you told me no," I say louder, refusing to be ignored.

"Lower your voice, young lady. For your information, you asked me to buy you a black push-up bra from

Victoria's Secret. I didn't really think it was appropriate for a fifth grader," Mom smarts off.

"Oh." I do remember the bra being black. Jentry makes a snorting noise and I'm pretty sure she just accidentally snorted some rice.

"If you really want to have this discussion, I went back and got you two training bras the next day. Of course, you had already taken it upon yourself to make your own."

Dad fidgets uncomfortably in his seat. Sean is laughing so hard that I'm just waiting for a snow pea pod to come out his nose. He is such a brat. He has always gotten to say or do whatever he wants. I'll show him.

"Mom, did you know Sean looks at porn on the family computer?"

"Grace!" my family shouts in unison. Jentry spits the water she had in her mouth into her napkin and tries hard not to bust out laughing. Dad takes a long swig of sake.

"You are in so much trouble when we get home, young man," Mom says, pushing her chair back and disappearing toward the bathroom.

"Thanks a lot, Graceless," Sean yells, stomping off in the opposite direction as Mom.

My stomach cramps up with guilt for busting Sean. He didn't know that I was trying to keep my age a secret. I guess the bra thing is kind of funny. I'm just so confused. I love my new life but a part of me realizes now how much I've missed my family.

"Hey, sisters," a cheery voice says, cutting through my

pity party. I look up to see Kai, a fellow Alpha, standing at our table. My stomach officially plummets to my ankles.

"Hey, Kai. Your hair looks adorable," Jentry says in an attempt to distract Kai, who is glancing over at my father.

"Thanks. I don't know why I even bothered since we are all just going to be hanging out in our pajamas later," she says, tossing her silky ebony locks over her shoulder.

"Yeah. Good times," Jentry says.

"These two are so rude," Kai says, holding her hand out to my father. "I'm Kai."

When she doesn't add, "their sorority sister" to the end of her introduction, my heart leaps. Dad will just think Kai called us sisters as an endearing term. He won't think anything of it.

"I'm Grace Kelly's father," Dad says, shaking Kai's hand.

"Nice to meet you, Mr. Cook. I'm sure we'll see you around the house soon," she laughs. "I'd better get." Dad looks confused, but Kai rushes off before he can ask her what she means. Mom and Sean pass Kai without realizing she was talking to us. The sudden dip in my oxygen level is threatening to make me pass out in my bowl of stir-fry. I do not have the temperament to live on the edge like this. Sometimes I just want to crawl back into my books and never come out.

"Your father and I will discuss your punishment at home. Let's not ruin our dinner," Mom says, hushing Sean, who is pleading for his computer time not to be completely revoked.

I'm trying to figure out how I can backtrack to get Sean out of trouble when I hear Kai's voice again.

"Sorry to interrupt everybody, but Grace Kelly, I just wanted to remind you to wear your pledge pin to the Alpha house tonight. I saw that you didn't have it on and I didn't want you to get in trouble."

• • •

We are back in my dorm room after our disastrous dinner. I am sitting in my plastic desk chair with my knees pulled up to my chest. Mom is pacing our floor while hanging up clothes I discarded earlier when I got dressed. Jentry is curled on her bed in the fetal position. Mom finally runs out of clothes and squats down next to my chair.

"I want you to know that I'm really proud of you," she says, brushing some stray strands of hair behind my ears. "But I can't help but be worried about how fast you're moving. You've never been very big on change and now, in one week, you've moved away from home, changed your appearance, and joined a sorority. And classes haven't even started yet. How are you going to handle all this?"

This is just like her to treat me like a baby. I'm practically a grown woman, well, kind of, except without a driver's license. So what if I can't vote, or buy lotto tickets, or drink legally. I'm still a grown up. Sort of.

"I think I'm holding up pretty well," I smart off.

"Where is all of this attitude coming from?" she asks, looking sad.

Is she serious? Does she really not take responsibility for me being so ill-prepared to interact with my peers?

"Why didn't you ever try to help me look better or feel better about myself?" I demand.

The stunned look on Mom's face sends a dart of pain shooting through my chest.

"Grace Kelly, you never wanted anything to do with clothes or makeup. Your books were the only things that ever mattered to you. I didn't know how to compete with that," she defends herself. "The time I took you to get contacts, you got hysterical and kept screaming the parts of the eye until we got escorted out of the store. After that I just quit trying. You've always been smarter than me so I figured you knew what was best." She stands back up and moves across the room.

I want to scream at her and tell her to quit making excuses. Then a memory floats up of an elderly security guard rushing us somewhere, and I can hear myself screaming, "Iris, cornea, retina."

"You took me for contacts?" I ask amazed.

"I tried. I even tried to get you to cut your hair but you didn't want anything to do with it. You didn't want anything to do with me either. You still don't."

"That's not true, Mom," I say weakly. Because as much as I don't want to admit it, she's right. I always took her attempts to take me shopping or just spend time with me as her way of trying to sabotage my learning. My grades never seemed important to her. I would hand her a report card filled with straight As and barely get a response; then Sean would get a C and she would practically scream with joy.

"I've never really known how to talk to you," Mom admits. "But I've always trusted you. So if you really think you can handle all of this," she says, gesturing around the dorm room, "then I'll take your word for it."

I nod numbly, hoping I know what I'm doing.

•   •   •

I'm still in shock that Mom didn't throw all my stuff in garbage bags and drag me out of the dorm by my newly highlighted hair. She trusts me. She has never said that to me before and she sure never acted like it. I told Mom that I needed to use the bathroom and that I would meet her at the van to say goodbye. But the truth is that I don't really want to say goodbye. I miss my family. I miss my room back home. I'm comfortable there. At home I don't have to worry about my makeup being perfect or that I don't trip and fall; I can just be myself. It's not that I'm acting like a different person for the Alphas, but with the legacy lie and my age hanging over my head, I always feel on guard. Not to mention watching my back so that Sloane doesn't trick me again.

I had to come in and sit on a closed toilet seat to calm myself down. The last thing I want to do after convincing my mom that I'm mature enough to handle college is go down to the car and start bawling when they leave. Which doesn't even make sense because I love it here. I just wish I could have both.

I take a few calming breaths and then make my way out of the dorm and toward the visitor parking lot.

"Grace Kelly. Over here," I hear a voice whisper from behind a tree. I walk toward the voice to see Aimee, a fellow Alpha, hunkered down spying on two girls.

"Aimee, what are you doing?"

"That's my ex-girlfriend and the ho she dumped me for. Look at her. She's not even cute. Got thunder thighs?" she says bitterly. Okay, I so don't have time for this. "Oh my God, they're coming this way," she says, hopping up.

"Act natural," I tell her, although I'm sure she's pretty much going to be labeled a stalker once her ex sees her hiding behind this tree.

"Kiss me," Aimee demands, suddenly in my face.

"Uh, no offense—"

"I've got *K*. Kiss me and I'll run back to the house and rip it down," she pleads, her ex closing in on us. I debate for a second, then remember the cheerleaders-with-rage issues I had to deal with earlier. This kiss thing seems like a pretty easy out. I close my eyes, push my lips out, and lean in Aimee's direction. Our lips touch and she wraps her arms around me. Her lips are soft and pillowy but nowhere near as dreamy as Charlie's. I wonder if it's weird that my second kiss is from a girl.

I guess Aimee's plan must have worked because her ex is yelling at me to get away from her. I open my eyes and instead of being scared that I may have pissed off a rather large girl, I'm more terrified when I see Sean's eyes peering back at me from the back of my parent's minivan.

I walk toward the van, relieved when I realize that my parents were so deep in discussion they had no idea that their daughter was experimenting with the same sex just a few feet away. Sean is rolling around in the backseat holding his sides from laughing so hard. He's such a little troll and now he has so much power over me.

"Hi," I say when Mom rolls down her window. I can tell she's been crying but she's trying really hard to cover it up.

"I'm sorry that we surprised you tonight. We won't do it again," Mom says.

I have never had a stronger urge to grab her and never let go. I know it is going to be a long time before I see her again because I'm just not strong enough to go home for a visit yet.

"We love you, Grace Kelly," Dad adds, blowing me a kiss.

"Don't do anything I wouldn't do, GK," Sean says, adopting Jentry's nickname for me, while wrapping his arms around himself acting like he is making out with someone.

"Mom, I'm not going to do anything to let you down," I say, and then remember the beer bong, the run-in with campus security, the panty slicing, and the making out with Charlie and then Aimee. Okay, so maybe I stretched the truth a little bit.

"She's going to make the right decisions, Marge," Dad defends me, raising his eyebrows at me in warning. Got it. If I get caught lying to them again, it won't be pretty.

"Give me a big hug, sis," Sean laughs, leaning out his back window. "I want naked pictures of Jentry emailed to me, ASAP, or I'll blow the lid off your lesbian lover," he whispers, holding up his cell phone. Great. He's got photographic proof. I'm so dead.

"Don't let yourself get too overwhelmed," Mom says, grabbing my hand.

Too late, I think, as I paste on a fake smile and watch my family drive away without me.

NINE

"Why the long face, Little Miss I-Graduated-High-School-Early?" Jentry asks, reminding me that I haven't exactly had a chance to explain why I lied to her about my age. After my parents left, I went back to my dorm room and got Jentry so that we could walk to the Alpha house together.

"Listen, Jentry. I'm really sorry about lying to you," I say, suddenly paranoid that maybe Jentry will be mad and rat me out to the Alphas.

"You didn't lie. You just didn't volunteer the information. I'm kind of proud of you in a sick way," she laughs.

"You aren't mad?" I ask, relieved.

"You were just looking out for yourself. I get it."

"What if the Alphas find out?"

"Why would they care?" she asks, confused.

"I don't know. I just don't want them thinking I'm too young."

"Well, then we just won't tell them," she says, smiling.

My stomach stops churning just knowing that, once again, Jentry is looking out for me. I guess maybe my whole family didn't drive away after all. I am so looking forward to a relaxing night at the house, I think, as Jentry opens the front door of the Alpha house. We dump our bags in the foyer and join the sisters in the great room. They are sprawled over furniture and the floor, chatting.

"Sit by me, Grace Kelly," a voice says. I can't tell who said it because all of the sisters are wearing pajamas and fuzzy slippers, talking excitedly. I practically have goose bumps, I'm so excited about my first overnight in the Alpha house. Being in the house with all the sisters is really helping me take my mind off missing my family.

"No, GK. Sit by me," Aimee says. I know I'm not imagining the googly eyes Aimee is directing my way when Jentry elbows me.

"Somebody's got a girl crush," she whispers. Yikes. I think I must have performed *K* a little too well.

"I know you're all excited, but everybody needs to take a seat so we can take care of some business before the sleepover starts," Lindsay says, walking to the front of the room. Jentry and I cop a squat right where we are. I finger my Alpha pin, which is back where it belongs, pinned to the collar of my pink silky pajama top. The cool metal of the pin is reassuring under my fingers.

"First off, I want to congratulate Grace Kelly for completing tasks *A*, *B*, *C*, *K*, *P*, and *Z*. Although *K* was sort of questionable," Lindsay says, throwing a dirty look toward

Aimee. "Grace Kelly has done everything the Alphas have asked of her and has completed tasks that have bettered our sorority and our campus." She beams at me. All the sisters start clapping, including Jentry, who is mouthing "What did you do for *K*?" I'm so lame that I'm afraid I might actually start crying. Being an Alpha means so much to me that I'm terrified the sisters will find out I'm a fake.

"Thanks, everybody," I manage to squeak out.

"Jentry and Sloane are moving right along, too," Lindsay says, gesturing to their missing letters.

It seems as though Sloane has miraculously recovered from the flu. She is looking vixen-like in a turquoise teddy and matching feather boa. I have no idea what would possess her to dress like that for a bunch of girls. She is weird/evil squared.

"Pledges, we have a certain number of volunteer hours that we have to maintain each month to be in good standing with National," Lindsay explains. "We need to decide where we are going to use our volunteer hours this month. Any suggestions?" Lindsay asks, poising her pen above her notebook.

"How about the soup kitchen?" someone volunteers.

"I'm not going back there. Some bum grabbed my butt last time," Juliet says, looking infuriated. We all start laughing.

"Okay, so the soup kitchen is out," Lindsay agrees. "How about Meals On Wheels?"

"No, way. I had a lady throw scalding hot meatloaf at

me because she thought I was trying to poison her," Jodi yells.

"Okay, then," Lindsay says, crossing something off her paper. "Is there any charity work we've done where someone hasn't been sexually harassed or assaulted by meat?"

Silence fills the room. I timidly raise my hand.

"This isn't kindergarten, Grace Kelly. Just say what's on your mind," Lindsay jokes.

"What about the animal shelter?" I ask, thinking it would be a blast to take care of animals. The sisters start chatting excitedly amongst themselves.

"That's a great idea, Grace Kelly. All in favor?" Lindsay asks. Every girl in the room shouts, "Aye."

Lindsay reaches up to the letters behind her. She yanks down the *V* and crumples it in her palm. "*V* for volunteer," she says, smiling. Sweet! Another letter done. Lindsay is the coolest sister ever.

"Hey, *V* was my letter," another sister starts to complain. Before Lindsay can respond, a loud crashing noise comes from the foyer. All the sisters scramble to their feet and head toward the sounds that are booming from the foyer. Jentry and I are nearly there when we hear a guy's voice yell out, "Panty raid." All the sisters start screaming and chasing after frat guys wearing ski masks and all black.

"This is like a bad '80s movie," Jentry laughs.

"What's going on?" I ask nervously.

"They're here for our panties. It's a really lame fraternity tradition," Jentry explains.

"What? No," I shake my head furiously, mortified at the thought of giving my underwear to a total stranger.

One of the panty raiders comes up behind her and scoops her up in his arms. It would be impossible not to recognize Ron's huge muscles underneath his disguise. Jentry pulls up the bottom part of his mask to expose his lips, then kisses him. I go back into the great room to give them some privacy and to escape the madness of all the sisters screaming that they aren't giving up their best Victoria's Secret panties just for a stupid gag.

"Give 'em up, Grace Kelly," a familiar voice whispers in my ear. My knees practically go weak hearing Charlie's voice. His chest is pressed against my back with his hands holding my arms to my sides.

"I don't live here. All my panties are at the dorm," I say, happy to have a legitimate excuse. Nothing would embarrass me more than having to hand over a pair of my new not-so-granny panties to Charlie except maybe handing over a pair of my old granny panties.

"Not all of them," he says, moving his hands dangerously close to my butt. I thought I was faint tonight with all the parent drama but that was nothing compared to what Charlie's touch does to me. The commotion in the foyer seems to have died down and it feels like we are all alone in the house.

"You've got to be kidding," I say weakly, knowing I would give him just about anything he wanted right now.

"I never kid when it comes to undergarments," he says. He releases one of my arms then uses his free hand to pull my hair off my neck while he starts kissing it. I lose myself in the feel of his hot breath and lips on my skin. Yelling and slamming doors yank me back to reality.

"Turn around," I demand. All I can see of his face is a giant grin and two smiling eyes peering back at me before he turns around. I yank my silky pajama bottoms and my underwear down quickly. My ankle gets caught on my underwear as I try to grab it, and I crash into the wall. Charlie snickers lightly. So much for being sexy. I ball up my underwear in my hand and then pull my pajama bottoms back on. I cannot believe that I am about to hand over my underwear to a guy I barely know. Ignoring the whole humiliation factor, this can't be sanitary.

I stuff them into his pocket and shove him toward the foyer before I chicken out. He whistles happily on his way out without ever looking back.

I crumple onto a leather chair, laughing. Thank God I had my new underwear on. I hear what sounds like a warrior cry come from the foyer, then the front door slams and the Omegas are gone.

"You look positively guilty," Jentry says, collapsing in another chair across from me. The skin around her mouth is red and splotchy from Ron's goatee whiskers.

"I just gave Charlie my underwear," I laugh.

"I should have known you'd pack a spare pair. I bet you were a kick ass Girl Scout, GK," she laughs.

"I didn't give him a spare pair," I tell her, trying to keep a straight face.

"Oh my God, I've created a monster," Jentry laughs.

"He is the most amazing kisser. Not that I have anything to compare it to besides Aimee, but that doesn't really count," I babble. As soon as I realize what I just said I slap my hand over my mouth in shock. Jentry is sitting straight up in the chair looking serious.

"Don't tell anybody I just told you that," I whisper, petrified that someone is going to find out that I accidentally told Jentry about one of my tasks.

"I know you really like this guy, GK, but you need to be careful," Jentry warns, not even hearing my slip about the *K* task.

I should have known that Charlie was too good to be true. "Does he have a girlfriend or something?" I ask, feeling devastated already.

"This is about you, GK, not him. You're underage and he could go to jail if you... you know," she whispers.

I bury my face in my hands and wonder what Google would tell me to do about all this mess I've gotten myself into.

• • •

Two days later I'm heading across campus, practically giddy. It's the first day of classes and I can hardly wait to get somewhere I feel comfortable. The only thing that would make this morning any better is if I had my trusty backpack. Jentry made me trade it in for a leather messenger bag, completely ignoring my ergonomic argument about shoulder strain.

Campus looks so much different with everyone here. I got used to wandering around, taking in the weathered brick buildings and not thinking about plowing into someone. Today the sidewalks are packed with fellow students looking sleepy while wearing iPods, drinking coffee, and straggling to class. I'm so glad that I thought to map out the route to my classes so that I'm not trying to find my way to unfamiliar buildings with these crowds. I make it safely to Mason Hall without incident.

I sneak in the double doors behind some guys I recognize as Omegas. I immediately think of Charlie, and start wondering what he did with my underwear. Before I know it, I'm forced into a giant throng of students headed down a long corridor. I start to panic, realizing I'm in the middle with no chance of escaping. Slowly students start to drop off as they dart into classrooms to the right and left of the corridor. Before long I'm alone, most people having already found their assigned classrooms.

I pull out my class schedule, scanning for my room number. I can't believe I was so focused on finding my way to the building that I never even considered that the inside of the building would be impossible to manage. My schedule says that Organic Chemistry is in Schroeder Auditorium. Auditorium? I'm starting to panic because no one else is around, but I haven't heard the bell ring yet, so I should be okay.

I fly dangerously down the hall, knowing that I am taking my life into my own hands. I round the corner only to be faced with another gigantic hallway. I notice two blondes twirling their hair and chatting by a drinking fountain.

"Excuse me? Can either of you tell me where Schroeder Auditorium is?"

The girls turn in my direction and I see the huge *Z*s across their T-shirts. Zetas. Their eyes immediately lock onto my Alpha pin. Uh, oh. I start to back slowly away. I recognize one of them from the locker room incident.

"Oh, sure. You just take these stairs," one of the Zetas says, pointing to a staircase. "And go up two flights of stairs. It will be right on your left." They smile brightly and I realize they don't recognize me without my zebra head.

"Thanks," I yell, bounding up the steps. I feel a little guilty about the whole mooning incident since they were so nice to me. I don't have time to worry about it though because I have to get to class. I make it to the third floor only to find it deserted. They lied to me. Of course they did. How could I be so naïve? I sink down into an empty chair next to a dark office. I don't bother to try and stop the tears from running down my cheeks. I feel so lost.

"Grace Kelly?" a familiar voice asks, and someone bends down in front of me.

"Lindsay?" I say, swiping at my cheeks furiously. "What are you doing here?"

"I'm Dr. Brown's TA this semester, which basically means I run to his office for him thirty times a day," she explains, rolling her eyes. "Let me guess. The Zetas told you your class was up here?"

I nod pitifully.

"Those bottom-feeders are famous for doing that every year. Just ignore them. Is something else wrong?" she pries.

"College is so intimidating. I just wish I knew what I was doing. And I think I miss my family," I say, opening up.

"Freshman year is tough for everybody. I went home every weekend for the first four months," she admits.

"Really?" I can't imagine self-assured, Alpha-president Lindsay being homesick.

"Yep, and I was eighteen, not sixteen," she says, stopping my heart. I meet her eyes and she smiles.

"I'm sorry I didn't tell you." A million thoughts rush through my mind. The biggest one wondering if the Alphas were going to kick me out of the sorority.

"It's okay. I probably wouldn't have told either."

"Are you going to kick me out of the sorority?" I ask, holding my breath.

"And cut loose the only child prodigy on campus? No way," she laughs.

"What about the sisters?"

"You can tell them when you're ready."

She gets to her feet and pulls me up. I feel lighter just knowing that I have one less secret to hide.

Lindsay helps me find Schroeder (which is actually pronounced Schrater, just to trip up frogs like me) Auditorium. I can't believe it when I see three hundred other people seated and waiting for the instructor to pass out the syllabus.

Lindsay also reminded me that there are no bells in college, so technically, I'm late. She also reminded me that in college no one really cares if you come to class. This is going to take some getting used to.

I slide into the top row trying to bring as little attention to myself as possible.

Someone passes me a crisp, white syllabus and I run my palm over it lovingly. I'm finally back in my element. The professor tells us that we aren't babies anymore and can read through it on our own time, then immediately starts lecturing. I retrieve a notebook from my bag along with a number-two pencil. I flip open the notebook and breathe in the scent of the fresh paper. The familiarity of these supplies has an almost Zen-like effect on me.

"I put your panties in a very special place," a voice whispers in my ear. I push my pencil so hard that the lead breaks. So much for Zen. I look over into Charlie's dimpled, smiling face.

"I almost stabbed you," I bluff, tossing the broken pencil into my bag and retrieving a fresh one. I can't help but notice the number-two pencil tucked behind Charlie's ear. I really want to ask him if he derives the same amount of satisfaction as I do watching his pencil waste away over the semester from all his hard work, but I don't.

"You're awfully hard core, Grace Kelly," he laughs, flipping open his notebook to a page filled with the three steps of free radical halogenation. I can't help but be jealous of his neatly drawn diagrams with their perfectly straight labels. Even if I had taken the time to work ahead, mine never would have turned out that well.

"Pay attention," he teases, focusing his attention back

to the professor. I try, but he smells so good, even better than my notebook. As our professor describes the initiation phase, I can't help but picture Charlie and me as the two free radicals spinning around each other, just waiting for a reaction to initiate things. I guess I could just lean over and kiss him. You can't get much more reactive than that.

I notice Charlie flipping to a blank page of his notebook. He jots something down, then slides it in my direction and bumps my shoulder with his. I try to ignore the sparks that are popping under my sleeve where he touched me. His paper says, "Wanna study tonight?" I nearly knock my own notebook off in shock. Organic Chemistry, Charlie, and me? Could there be a better threesome? I get ready to scribble down an eager "Yes" when I remember that I have to be at the Alpha house tonight. Bummer. I write "Busy," but offer him a smile. He cocks his head to one side, examining me, then turns his attention back to the professor.

As much as I love learning about molecules and their complex relationships, my mind keeps floating back to the sisters and my relationship with them. Lindsay was so cool about my age. I wonder if I could tell her the truth about Edwina Fay and she would understand? I want to be honest with the sisters but I can't stand the thought of being kicked out of the sorority. I just can't take the chance of telling them I lied about being a legacy.

"A dollar for your thoughts," Charlie says, holding out a crisp one-dollar bill.

"Huh? What?" I ask, noticing that everyone around

us is already standing up and collecting their stuff. I can't believe I completely spaced out during my first lecture.

"You just looked so deep out there that I didn't think a penny would get me much." He laughs easily, then jams the money back into his cargo shorts.

"I guess I'm still adjusting to college." I slip my notebook into my bag and carefully tuck my pencil into a side pocket.

"That pin looks good on you," Charlie says, admiring my Alpha pledge pin. I reach up to my collar and spin the smooth gold pin between my fingers. I wonder if I will ever get used to being an Alpha? Maybe I shouldn't until all of my tasks are completed.

"Thanks," I say nervously, just remembering the bombshell Jentry laid on me the other night about Charlie getting in trouble for dating me. The last thing I want to do is stop our flirtation, if that's what it is, but I also don't want Charlie getting into trouble.

"See ya around," he says casually, hopping over me. He exits the auditorium, his tanned, muscular legs taking the steps two at a time. Sigh. That's one free radical I'd love to collide with.

· · ·

A few days have passed, but the memory of Charlie's legs bounding from the auditorium hasn't.

"What am I going to do?" I ask Jentry, while emailing my paper for English class to my instructor. If only my situation with Charlie was as easy as my assignments have been so far.

Jentry is sitting cross-legged on her bed bent over her psychology book like it is the most fascinating thing she has ever read. She has a pile of neon-colored highlighters next to her and every so often she will grab a specific color and highlight her text. I've never understood how outlining words in a different color helps people learn better, but to each their own I guess. She is concentrating so hard that she doesn't even hear me. I decide to leave her alone and boot up my laptop.

I pull up the Omega website just so that I can see Charlie's picture. In the picture he's sitting on the roof of the frat house, proudly sporting the horseshoe-looking symbol for Omega on his bare chest. I used to think that girls who spent all their time drooling over guys were just lower on the evolutionary food chain than normal people, but now I kind of get it. Blowing Charlie off is going to be the hardest thing I've ever done. I thought about just telling him the truth and letting him decide for himself, but I figure the fewer people who know about my age, the better. I successfully dodged him yesterday in chemistry lab, but it wasn't easy. Thankfully our lecture is in the auditorium so it will be much easier to hide from him.

My computer chimes that I have a new email, so I toggle off the Omega website to my email account. The highlighted sender's name is "Anonymous." In the subject field it says, "*H*, *D*, and *S*." I click on the email to open it and all it says is "Third floor library, Wednesday, Eight p.m." Thank goodness I have two days to rest. I never realized how much the tasks, classes, and all the extracurriculars for the sorority would take out of me. Not to mention the extra time I have to spend on my hair, makeup, and clothes now. But I guess it is a small price to pay to be an Alpha.

I delete the top-secret task email and move on to the next one, which is from Sean. There is no subject. When I double click to open it, my screen fills up with a picture of me kissing Aimee. In giant bold letters underneath it says, "12 hours left." I really thought Sean was kidding about the blackmail. Like I don't have enough to worry about.

"Who took that?" Jentry shrieks from behind me.

"That would be my disgusting troll of a little brother," I admit, spinning around in my chair to face her.

She puts her hands over her mouth in horror but her eyes are laughing. "That midget is truly diabolical. You better give him what he wants," she laughs.

I avert my eyes and get very busy straightening the pens sitting in my plastic Alpha cup.

"Oh, no. Why do I have the feeling that I'm part of his little scheme?" she asks.

"He would never show Mom," I say, knowing that my voice doesn't sound believable even to myself.

"But if he did..." she trails off. "What does he want?" she sighs.

"Naked pictures... of you," I tell her, disgusted. How Sean and I came from the same gene pool is beyond me.

"I'm not doing nude for anybody but Playboy, but I'll

give him a couple of shots of me in my bikini. That should tide him over," she says, moving toward her dresser.

"You really don't have to do this. I mean, you've done so much for me already," I plead, feeling horribly guilty.

"I do have to do this. I can't imagine being here without you," she grins, slipping into her bikini. "Let's do this," she says, handing me her digital camera.

I am going to owe her so big for this.

•   •   •

It's Wednesday morning and I am skulking around the edges of the auditorium looking for Charlie. Luckily I'm here before he is, so I choose a seat in the farthest corner away from where we normally sit. I tuck my hair into the ball cap I borrowed from Jentry and hunker down into my seat. I know I should just talk to him, but I don't think I could look him in the eyes and tell him I didn't want to see him anymore. I figure if I blow him off long enough, he'll lose interest.

I peek over my shoulder to see Charlie at the top of the auditorium looking around. He shrugs and takes a seat in our normal row. He tucks his hair behind his ear while removing a notebook from his backpack. I'm glad I'm sitting down because just that simple gesture practically makes me swoon.

I flip open my notebook, determined to give my full attention to Professor Pike. Between my Alpha tasks, keeping Mom off my back, Sean's blackmail, and just keeping up with this new look, which requires way more maintenance than I ever would have thought possible, I don't have time for a boyfriend. I'm not even going to think about Charlie anymore. Satisfied with my decision, I write today's date at the top of a fresh notebook page and ready myself to soak up some new chemistry knowledge.

"How many elements are in the periodic table?" Professor Pike's voice booms over the auditorium.

"One hundred seventeen," several voices yell out. I grip the edge of my desktop to resist the urge to scream out. Surely someone else in this room knows that element 118, while it hasn't existed for more than a few milliseconds, does exist after being created by American and Russian scientists.

"Come on, people," Professor Pike grumbles, obviously disgusted. I swear I could almost hear crickets chirping outside, the auditorium is so quiet. I squirm around in my seat restlessly. A girl next to me eyeballs me, probably afraid I'm about to have an accident. I can't help it though. It is physically painful not to answer Professor Pike's question. How can no one know this? Do these people not have www.dailyscience.com bookmarked? The word is just about to escape my lips when I hear someone else yell something out.

A garbled answer echoes through the otherwise silent auditorium.

"Was that English?" Professor Pike responds.

"Ununoctium is the one hundred eighteenth element," Charlie yells out, unclenching the pencil in his teeth.

I don't hear how Professor Pike responds to Charlie's correct answer because I have melted into a puddle of girl drool in my chair.

• • •

Later that night, I'm sitting alone at a table on the third floor of the library, engrossed in my American Government text, when I hear several "pssts." I look up to see three of my sorority sisters peeking around the corner, gesturing me to follow them into a restroom. I slam the fat textbook closed, shove it in my backpack, and sneak off to find out what my next tasks are.

I knock quietly on the restroom door and someone pulls me into the dark bathroom. A deadbolt locks behind me then the lights are flipped on. These girls aren't playing around.

"We've been wronged and we need your help," Jessica says, escorting me to have a seat on a closed toilet seat in the handicapped stall.

"He told us we were stupid," Mari says furiously. I don't know who they are talking about and I don't know Mari very well, but I heard her spouting baseball statistics the other day, and anybody with a mind for memorization like that is far from stupid.

"Who is 'he'?" I ask.

"Dean Stone," Allison finally pipes up, her cheeks flushing just saying his name.

"The dean of this college, Dean Stone?" I ask, hoping I'm confused.

"He's a pompous ass and we hate him. He's always insinuating that the Alphas are a bunch of airheads," Jessica rants.

"He actually pulled me out of an advanced statistics class because he felt it would be over my head," Mari adds distractedly while pulling on the end of the roll of toilet paper.

"We need you to humiliate him the same way he has humiliated us," Allison tells me.

"But he's the dean. The dean of the college," I say stupidly. "What could I possibly do to humiliate him?"

All three smile wickedly at me as they start to whisper their master plan.

• • •

"Booth for one please," I tell the perky hostess at the campus sports bar/restaurant. A banner above me tells me that tonight is ten-cent buffalo wing night, which explains the mounds of discarded chicken bones in the middle of most of the packed tables.

"We don't have any booths left, but I can get you a seat at the bar," she tells me sweetly, her eyes zeroing in on my Alpha pledge pin.

I smile at her, realizing that I'll be less obvious sitting at a crowded bar than in a booth by myself anyway. She gestures toward the bar and I head that way. Without being too obvious, I try to scan the room for Dean Stone. I still can't get over how he is so lame he would hang out all night at a campus sports bar to play trivia. But when I spot him hunched over his royal blue controller, his eyes are locked to one of the thirty flat screens hanging from the ceiling, ignoring his barbeque ribs and onion rings. It's pretty obvious that the girls weren't kidding when they said he took his unofficial title as "Best Trivia Player Ever" very seriously. I slide onto the bar stool, practically giddy about stealing his title away from him.

"What'll ya have, sweet cheeks?" a male bartender with a nose ring asks me. My cheeks are suddenly on fire, and it's not because of the affectionate greeting he gave me. My palms start to sweat as I spy the bottles of liquor behind him sparkling like jewels. I glance nervously around at my bar mates. They are all sophisticatedly tossing back fancy-looking mixed drinks and beers I can't pronounce. I'm way out of my league here. I might as well have "underage loser" written on my forehead. The bartender is waiting patiently for my reply. I have to say something. I blurt out the first thing that comes to mind.

"Can I get a Shirley Temple please?" I force out, then pretty much want to run for the door. Of all the things to ask for. I'm going to blow this task before I even start it. And it isn't like nobody will notice me, considering the girls made me dress like a walking Alpha billboard. I'm wearing Mari's low-rise jeans that she sewed Alpha patches on, a pink Alpha tank top with my pledge pin stuck to it, and a baby blue Alpha ball cap. The bartender looks me up and down and I'm pretty sure he's going to announce to the entire bar how incredibly lame I am.

"Do you want cherries with that?" he asks, grabbing a frosted glass from a freezer under the bar.

I nod my head, not trusting my voice. He busies himself making my drink and I scan the bar inconspicuously. I see the trio I'm representing tonight wave giddily from their corner booth. They can hardly wait for Dean Stone to get pummeled and for him to figure out it's the Alphas who did it.

The bartender sets my delicious-looking drink in front of me with the same flourish as if he were presenting a margarita with actual tequila in it. He winks at me as I pull out one of the cherries and pop it into my mouth.

"Hey, can I get one of those game controllers?" I ask, noting that one of the big screens says a new game is about to begin. He produces a blue controller from behind the bar and turns it on for me.

I type in GK under player's name. This will be changed later, once I've beaten Stone. I may be nervous about being only sixteen and sitting at a bar, but I'm not nervous at all about going up against Dean Stone in a game of wits. My mom has had me under lock and key for the last sixteen years and I've racked up a ton of useless trivia knowledge.

My name flashes on the screen with a score of zero. I join about ten other players, some who look to be pretty serious, others who answer a question here and there between buffalo wings. Dean Stone is in first place with 5,000 points already. He must have gotten here when the doors opened.

And I thought I was a loser. I see him perk up a bit when he sees someone new has joined the game and I watch him scan the room trying to find his newest victim. I hide my controller in front of me and act very interested in my drink. He forgets all about me when the first new question flashes on the screen.

It takes me just a second to get the hang of the game. The questions are multiple choice on pretty much any subject. You are given four answers and clues about the answer. The faster you answer the question, the more points you get. Easy enough. With a little luck, Dean Stone will get tripped up on a few questions and I'll be able to gain on him in a hurry.

The first question pops up. What was Margaretha Zelle's nickname? My fingers fly to the number three for the answer of Mata Hari. Thanks to Mrs. Morford, my high school history teacher, I know that Margaretha/Mata was executed by a firing squad in 1917 after being accused of being a German spy. I sip on my drink while waiting for the answer and the new scores. I see other players continuously changing their answers with the additional clues that are given. Finally the time is up and the new scores flash on the screen. I am the only one who answered the question fast enough to get one thousand points. Dean Stone must have waited for the first clue because he only got six hundred points. I hear the Alpha trio squealing for joy. Dean Stone scans the room for his competition. I turn back to the controller, laughing, and await the next question.

I try not to laugh while answering the ridiculously

easy question, "If 40 percent of the people at an event are women and 20 percent of the people at the event are left-handed, then, at most, what percentage are right-handed men?" Hello. Sixty percent. The trio looks worried but I flash them a smile. Dean Stone looks confident and when the screen shows that we were the only ones to score a thousand points I know why. This might take a little longer than I thought.

The screen pops up with the question, "Which letter does not appear on the periodic table?" I push two for *J* so quickly that I knock my drink over. I grab the controller so no pop spills on it. The bartender wipes up the mess with a bar rag.

"Jesus, you just can't go anywhere without making a spectacle of yourself, can you?" a familiar evil voice says from behind me. I spin around to come face-to-face with Sloane, who is looking like she just jumped off the pages of a fashion magazine with her low-cut turquoise stretch top and perfectly fitting jeans. She has been suspiciously absent around the dorm for a few days. Jentry and I had been hoping she'd dropped out of school. I should have known I'd never be that lucky.

"What can I say, Sloane? I'm not perfect like you," I smart off, tired of being afraid of her and feeling sort of falsely confident, being totally in my element with the trivia questions.

"I'll tell you who's perfect. That Omega specimen over there," she says wickedly, pointing toward a table of Omegas I hadn't noticed. Charlie is doing some damage to a basket of wings and doesn't seem to notice me. The bartender sets a fresh drink in front of me.

"Good luck with that," I shrug, turning back around. I could almost swear I can feel heat on my back from where she is staring holes into me. I pop another cherry in my mouth and wait for the next question. A few seconds later, I hear the click of Sloane's stilettos as she storms off. I let out the breath I didn't realize I'd been holding.

I can't believe she is still holding such a grudge over a little bit of marinara sauce. I really thought she would be over it by now. And I thought I was immature. Now she thinks she is going to make a play for Charlie. Not that he is mine to be stolen away or anything, since I'm blowing him off, but it is pretty funny that she thinks he would ever go for someone like her. Charlie would see through Sloane in two seconds.

I answer the next four trivia questions perfectly and am gaining on Dean Stone's score. Only three more questions are left in this round and if I answer them perfectly and Dean Stone hesitates, I'll become the top scorer. I wink at my sisters, who are nervously fidgeting around in their booth.

The next question pops up: "24 = h. in a d., you would say 'hours in a day.' See if you can figure this one out: 206 = b. in the h.b." 206 bones in the human body! I quickly touch number one to choose the correct answer. This is the easiest task I've had so far. I almost feel guilty that it is worth three letters. The score comes up showing that I now have a small lead on Dean Stone because he didn't score any points on the last question.

"I almost didn't recognize you," Charlie says from behind me. I drop my controller and it slams on top of the bar, smashing my finger in the process.

"Hey, Charlie," I say, not turning around. I start playing with the huge pile of cherry stems I've amassed.

"Have you been trying to hide from me?" he asks, sounding sort of sad.

"That's crazy," I answer back, but even to me my voice sounds flat.

"Is this about your panties?" he asks sincerely. For the first time since I sat down, the girl next to me looks over with a smirk on her face. Why did he have to bring that up?

"No, it isn't," I say, spinning around to shush him. The look on his face stops me from saying anything else. He's upset. At me.

"Can we go somewhere and talk?" he asks.

"We are somewhere and we are talking," is what my mouth says, but my heart is nearly beating out of my chest just being so close to him. His adorable face falls and I'm about to cave when Mari and Jessica rush up excitedly.

"I knew you were smart but this is amazing!" Jessica says.

"Charlie, isn't our new pledge amazing?" Mari asks, winking at Charlie. He smiles goofily, caving in that adorable dimple of his. I look away so that I don't get sucked into it.

"Yeah, not only is she the niece of the most famous cosmetics CEO in the whole world, but she's like a total brainiac, too," Jessica gushes.

"Edwina Fay," Mari and Jessica say in unison, then follow up with a sigh. I would be laughing hysterically if the mere mention of Edwina's name didn't practically make me break into hives at remembering my huge lie.

"Are they saying that you are Edwina Fay Brighton's niece?" Charlie asks. I nod, positive that not only does Charlie have no clue who Edwina Fay is but that he is probably just trying to make small talk.

The look he gives me forces me to look away, and even the girls must realize something is going on because they scoot back to their booth in a hurry. How in the world am I supposed to concentrate with all this boy drama going on? I signal for the bartender to bring me another drink. I'm hitting the kiddie cocktails hard tonight.

"You're a wolf in sheep's clothing, Grace Kelly," Charlie says mysteriously.

I laugh to myself, thinking that nothing could be further from the truth. I'm about to ask him what he means when I see the next trivia question come up on one of the other television screens. I hurriedly spin around and pick the correct answer. I barely make it before the first clue is given and points start being deducted.

"Whew, that was close," I say, turning back around to Charlie. But Charlie is gone. He's back over at his table, and to my ultimate horror, Sloane is leaning in so close to him that he's got a straight line of vision down her shirt. He doesn't look nearly as miserable as he just did a moment ago. Tears fill my eyes and I spin back around so no one notices the look on my face. I can't even begin to hide my pain at seeing Sloane invade Charlie's personal space.

Maybe she is just asking him where the bathroom is or something. The final question pops onscreen, and for a second, I forget all about Sloane and Charlie and answer it correctly. I'm so confident that I picked the right answer that if I was on *Jeopardy*, I'd wager everything I had.

Since this is the last question, the screen doesn't automatically tell the right answer. It takes a commercial break then comes back to announce the overall winner. I change my player name to what the trio agreed on so that when my name flashes across the screen in huge letters, Dean Stone won't have any doubt who beat him. I sneak a peek at Dean Stone, who has his eyes glued to the screen. I notice for the first time that the bar has gotten quieter and I can actually hear the music. Then I notice everyone seems to be staring at the screen.

I hear the cheers go up and see Dean Stone rush from the building, and I don't even have to look to the screen to know what it says. STONESUXALPHAZROK. My trio of sisters practically bum-rush me off my bar stool. They each take turns hugging me and it feels amazing to be three letters closer to being a real Alpha. But when I see Sloane give me a half-wave as Charlie escorts her out of the bar, I don't feel quite so amazing anymore.

TEN

The last four weeks have been filled with cramming for tests, volunteering at the pet shelter with the Alphas, successfully dodging Charlie and Sloane, or Chloane as Jentry and I refer to them, and knocking out tasks *G*, *I*, *M*, *N*, *Q*, *U*, *X*, and *Y*. I feel like I haven't had a moment to breathe. Now that I do, I don't know quite what to do with myself. I prop my pillows against my cinderblock wall and lean back. Jentry is inputting something into her BlackBerry and doesn't look like she would hear me even if I tried to interrupt her. I flip open my Organic Chemistry text and try to read ahead.

After reading the same paragraph four times, I slam it shut and toss it on the end of my bed. I sigh heavily but Jentry still doesn't bite. I'm restless but I can't figure out why. I used to get like this before a big test and Mom would make me a giant mug of hot chocolate with tons of fluffy marshmallows. I could sure go for a mug of that right now. That instant crap in the cafeteria just doesn't compare to Mom's.

Then I realize that I can't remember the last time I talked to my mom. Somehow her daily calls dropped off and I didn't even notice. What if something bad happened and nobody thought to call me? I bolt off my bed and grab my cell phone off my desk. My heart is pounding with every number I punch in. It seems to take forever to connect the call. I finally understand what people mean when they say their life flashed in front of their eyes.

"What up, narc?" Sean greets me, obviously still not quite over me busting out his online porn habit.

"Where's Mom?" I practically scream at him. Jentry stops texting, her thumbs posed in mid-air as concern clouds her features.

"She's at work," Sean answers back testily.

"What do you mean? Mom doesn't work."

"She does now. She got a job at the library. You aren't the only one with a life, you know?" Sean smarts off.

"The library? Really?" I can't remember the last time I saw Mom curled up with a good romance novel. I had almost forgotten about her passion for fiction.

"Unless you're calling to say Jentry is sending me some new skin pics, I've got stuff goin' on."

"Just tell Mom I called," I trail off. Sean grunts something unintelligible, then hangs up.

"My mom got a job," I tell Jentry, still shocked. My mind knows that a part-time job at the library isn't a big deal, but my heart is banging around in my chest, confused. My mom has always been at home waiting for me. I guess I thought she always would be.

"That's a good thing," Jentry reminds me, going back to her phone.

Yeah, a good thing.

• • •

"We should probably bolt," Jentry says a few minutes later, glancing at our alarm clock. I don't know what she is referring to until I see her grab her bookbag. Alpha study hours.

I throw some books into my bag and follow Jentry out the door. My mind is still on Sean and Mom as Jentry locks our door. We start down the hall quietly but I'm soon stopped dead in my tracks by Sloane's bulletin board. A huge hot-pink heart covers the entire board and inside it is written "Sloane + Charlie."

"What is she? Ten?" Jentry laughs, pulling me away.

"It doesn't matter. I couldn't date him anyway," I lie, trying not to cry.

"It does matter because you liked him. And he liked you. He's probably just trying to get back at you."

It made me feel a little better to hear Jentry say she knew Charlie liked me. At least I hadn't imagined it after all. Not that it really matters.

"So what did my creepy little boyfriend have to say?" Jentry changes the subject as we walk across campus to the Alpha house.

"I think my mom is getting a life."

"I think she always had one, she just forgot for a little bit," Jentry adds. "She's not so bad. And I kind of like her inspirational emails."

"She sends those to you, too?" I ask, amazed.

"Every morning like clockwork." She laughs, but something tells me she wasn't lying when she said she enjoyed them.

"This is a good thing, GK," Jentry reassures me again, squeezing my arm, before opening the front door to the Alpha house.

All the active sisters are here already. They must have had an actives-only meeting before study hours. I really can't wait until initiation to find out all the Alphas' secrets. All the girls are sprawled in various positions on the furniture and the floor. I love the nights when we all get together and study. Being in the house has such a calming effect on me, unless one of the sisters brings up Edwina Fay. Jentry and I settle down together and rest our backs on an overstuffed pillow.

"Okay, there's just a little bit of business tonight, then we have to get busy studying so we can keep showing Dean Stone how smart the Alphas are," Lindsay says, winking at me. "First off, everyone has done an excellent job fulfilling their volunteer hours. The staff at the animal shelter wanted you to know how much they appreciate all your hard work." She pauses to give the sisters time to let up a little cheer.

"I also wanted to point out that our three pledges only

have eight more tasks to complete. If you haven't discussed your task with them, please do so soon. And last, I just accepted an invitation to the Omega Tau Nu's Monster Mash." The sisters go crazy with excitement, but I'm a little less enthused thinking about partying with Chloane. Hopefully I won't recognize them in their costumes.

"Does anyone have new business?" Lindsay asks. I notice someone's hand dart up energetically out of the corner of my eye. I glance over to see Sloane sitting cross-legged and bouncing around like she has to pee.

"Yes, Sloane," Lindsay says, acknowledging her.

"I hope this is okay but I ordered Double Happy, my treat," she says giddily.

Cheers go up from everyone but Jentry and me because we know Sloane is just trying to kiss up to the actives by buying Chinese food.

"The only thing is," Sloane continues, "I forgot my driving glasses so I was wondering if Grace Kelly would mind taking my car to get the food." Her eyes seem to twinkle with evil as they meet my panic-stricken ones.

"Sure, no problem," I force out, ignoring the jolt of ephephrine to my heart at the thought of not having a driver's license.

• • •

A few minutes later, I'm in the Alpha parking lot behind the house. I click the unlock button on the keypad and a beep and flashing lights come from a luxury SUV that rivals the size of the bus I rode last year. This is going to be bad. Very bad.

I always meant to take driver's ed and get my license but more interesting class choices always seduced me away. I've been perfectly fine letting Mom chauffeur me around.

I slide into the buttery leather of the driver's seat and hunt around for the seat adjustment. I can do this. If Tommy Crawley can learn how to drive, so can I. Tommy was the only eighth grader with a driver's license because he had flunked so many times. This cannot be hard. I put the key in the ignition and turn it. The radio blares, nearly giving me a stroke. I fumble with the knob to turn it down. I find the lights with no problem.

I jam my foot on the brake and move the control thingy from park to reverse. I hold my breath while I gently ease up on the brake. The SUV seems to leap backward so I jam on the brake again, nearly giving myself whiplash. I can do this. I can do this. I ease up on the brake again and slowly crawl out of the parking space. I crank the wheel too quickly, almost crashing into Lindsay's VW. I slam on the brakes just in time. I hear one of the back doors opening, then see Jentry diving onto the floorboard.

"What are you doing?" I exclaim.

"Saving somebody the trouble of scraping you off the pavement," she says, ducking down. "Now stop talking and drive us down to the Zeta house," she demands, staying hunkered down.

I put the car in drive and pull forward a tiny bit, then back up, and finally make it out of the space. I drive slowly through the lot, alternating the brake and the gas with my left and right feet. I inch out near the main road in front of the Alpha house. Dozens of headlights are coming in my direction.

"I can't do this," I whine.

"You just have to wait until its all clear, then pull out slowly. The Zeta house is only a few hundred feet away and then I'll take over," she says calmly.

"She's watching," I say, spotting Sloane peeking out of an upstairs window. "She knows. That's why she did this."

"About your age? Nah, how would she know? Besides, Lindsay already knows so it doesn't matter."

Jentry's right. Sloane doesn't have anything on me. I'm sure she was expecting me to fess up to only being sixteen and not having a driver's license yet, but I surprised her by calling her bluff and taking her car. She's probably scared now that I'll wreck her precious car. The street is finally clear so I carefully pull out. I turn the wheel a little too quickly, which startles me so I jam on the brake, then the gas, causing the SUV to buck.

"I'm getting carsick," Jentry yells. "Keep your foot off the brake unless somebody runs in front of you."

I follow her instructions but keep my left foot hovering over the brake, just in case. I continue down the street, never going above fifteen miles per hour. Joggers are passing me.

"You drive worse than my grandma and she's got cataracts," Jentry laughs.

I ignore her and continue slowly up the road until I

see the Zeta sorority house. Several girls are standing outside when I inch into their driveway. I check to make sure the doors are locked because this doesn't seem like the best place for two Alpha pledges to be.

"Pull to the back of the house," Jentry says, sitting up.

I follow her instructions, pulling alongside several other cars almost identical to Sloane's. I let out a breath I didn't realize I was holding as I put the car into park. I scoot over to the passenger seat and Jentry jumps in the front. She is just about to put the car in reverse when I hear a knock on my window. I scream. I look over to see a brunette with a Zeta tank top standing next to the car. She has a very confused look on her face that quickly turns to anger as her eyes spy my Alpha pin.

"Get out of the car," she yells at us.

Jentry peels out of the driveway and back onto the main road leaving the girl in her dust. She tries running after us but gets winded pretty quickly.

"Holy crap, those girls are crazy," I laugh, wondering if my heart can take any more tonight.

"I told you," Jentry reminds me.

She turns up the radio and before long we are cruising through campus without a care. I'm feeling relaxed for the first time in a few days. Then I see red-and-blue flashing lights in the side mirror.

Jentry must have noticed them at the exact same time because she is already signaling to pull off the road.

"Oh my God, Jentry," I say, my palms already sweating.

"Just be cool, GK. I didn't do anything wrong," she whispers between gritted teeth. She pushes the button to open her window and smiles at the officer.

"Both of you, out of the car now," he demands, shining his flashlight into the car. We both do as he says and get out of the car. We meet at the back of the SUV where a second officer is waiting. My heart rate dips a little when I realize these guys are just campus security pulling us over in their souped-up golf cart, but it spikes again when I recognize one of the officers from the Alpha party that almost got busted. I keep my head down, hoping he doesn't recognize me.

"We got an anonymous tip that this vehicle was driving erratically. We have reason to believe you are driving under the influence of alcohol," he tells Jentry. Those damn Zetas called in an anonymous tip. They do not fight fair.

"I haven't had a drop to drink tonight," Jentry defends herself angrily.

"Good, then you won't mind taking a field sobriety test, will you?" the familiar officer smarts off.

"Bring it on," Jentry fires back. So much for playing it cool.

"Recite the alphabet. Backwards," the first cop says. Will these guys never learn?

"Actually Officer Frank, I think we need a different test. Her partner in crime is a crafty one and knows that like the back of her hand, so I'm sure this one isn't much different." My cheeks explode into flames when I realize that he recognized me.

• • •

A half-hour later Jentry waves goodbye to the officers and starts driving to Double Happy. The sisters probably think we ran away.

"It's a good thing I wasn't driving," I say relieved.

"Yeah, no kidding. There is no way you could have pulled off walking in a straight line while touching your nose," Jentry laughs.

I swat her arm playfully then collapse back into the luxurious leather seat. I can hardly wait to get back to the sorority house for a relaxing night of movies and food.

Wait a minute...

"She set me up," I blurt out, bolting up in my seat.

"Huh?" Jentry asks confused.

"Sloane called the cops, not the Zetas. She wanted me to get in trouble so that the Alphas would kick me out."

"But how would she know you didn't have a driver's license even if she did know you were only sixteen?" Jentry counters.

She has a point. "I don't know." I admit.

"Plus, you were driving her car, so she could have gotten in trouble too, and if you would have gotten caught it would have made the Alphas look bad. She wouldn't risk that," Jentry says confidently.

I guess she's right, but I still can't shake the feeling that there is more to it than that.

"You're just stressed. You'll feel better after spending the night at the house," she assures me.

She's right. I am stressed. Between my parents, the Alphas, and my classes, I feel like I'm juggling chain saws. I just hope that none of them come crashing down on me.

• • •

The next morning I'm no less stressed. I slam my laptop shut, even though I know I shouldn't treat it like that. I can't help it. The deadline to turn in my application for next spring's science fair is less than four weeks away and I can't think of a single worthy idea.

"Ron and I are dressing up like ketchup and mustard for the Monster Mash. I've always wanted to be a condiment for Halloween," Jentry says, obviously trying to get my mind on other things.

"That's nice," I say distantly. What costume I'm going to wear is the farthest thing from my mind. So far I've just been trying to deal with the fact that I will have to spend an entire evening with Chloane. Okay, not exactly with them, but in the same vicinity.

"You're going as Princess Grace," Jentry tells me. I laugh at her suggestion. "What? Check out your legs. You don't have one bruise on them," she points out.

I look down and realize she's right. I can't remember one accident I've had for several weeks. I've come a long way since I started school. My cell rings and my parents' phone number flashes on the display screen. It's about time. I've left a thousand messages lately. It's like my family has forgotten all about me.

"Hello, Mother," I say formally. I might as well start practicing talking properly if I'm going to dress up as a princess.

"Hello, Grace Kelly. How are you?" Mom asks cheerfully.

"Why haven't you called me back?" I demand.

"I'm sorry, sweetie. My job is keeping me pretty busy."

"It's like you don't even care about me anymore," I whine. Jentry gives me a strange look, which I ignore.

"Sweetheart, don't be silly. We are all really excited for you to come home for Thanksgiving."

"Don't you even care about my grades or anything?"

"I've never had to worry about your grades. Why would I start now?" Mom asks.

I don't say anything but Mom doesn't seem to pick up on my silence.

"How's Jentry?" Mom asks, changing the subject.

"Fine," I answer sharply.

Jentry makes a swiping motion across her neck but I ignore that, too.

"How's it going at the sorority?"

Like she really cares. She probably hopes I'll get kicked out. "You don't have to pretend you're okay with it, Mom."

"I think it's wonderful that you are making friends. My only concern was that you might get a bit overwhelmed."

"Well, I'm not," I huff. Why can't she just realize that I'm not an awkward little girl anymore? And if she was so concerned about me being overwhelmed, you think she would have returned my call a little sooner.

"It's getting cooler. I thought maybe we could run your sweaters up to you some night," Mom suggests.

I grip my phone tight with frustration. She just wants to come up here and spy on me. Wouldn't she be surprised to see how well I'm handling everything? I don't even know how to respond. So I don't. I hang up. I know hanging up on my mom isn't very mature, but she didn't give me any choice. She has to realize that she can't control me anymore.

• • •

Jentry looks at me, dumbfounded. "Did you just hang up on your mom?"

"She was wanting to bring me my sweaters. What a lame excuse to check up on me," I defend myself.

"It must really suck having people who care about you," Jentry smarts off, grabbing her BlackBerry while storming out of our room.

I sit cross-legged on my bed, dumbfounded. Just when I think I'm getting things right—not being so dependent on my parents, not being such a klutz, fitting in with all the sisters—I go and do something to drive away the one person who has helped me get here. I have a feeling that Jentry's blow-up isn't completely about the way I talked to my mom, but has something to do with her not talking to her own mom. I'm going to give her some time to vent, then try to patch things up. But first, I need to call Mom back.

I dial our home phone number and Sean picks up. Ugh. I am not really in the mood to talk to the little extortionist.

"Let me talk to Mom," I say.

"You made her cry, you big jerk," Sean yells at me. "She was doing so good, then you had to go and hang up on her."

"I didn't mean to," I say, feeling horrible.

"It doesn't feel very good, does it?" he asks, slamming the phone down.

• • •

Two hours later I find Jentry on her favorite bench on the quad.

"Peace offering?" I ask, offering her a pumpkin spice latte. She looks up and grabs the drink. I sit down on the bench next to her. I take a few sips of my own coffee and take in the red, yellow, and orange shades that the leaves on campus have turned. I just love it when the leaves lose their chlorophyll. The hot coffee does a good job of warming me up. I hadn't realized how chilly it had gotten when I left the dorm in just jeans and an oxford. It is hard to believe that I was in this same spot nearly two months ago when Jentry begged me to rush with her. Now I'm eight short tasks away from becoming a full-fledged Alpha and having everything I want.

"I'm not really mad at you," Jentry admits.

"I know. You were right though. I shouldn't take my

mom for granted. I know she loves me. I guess now that I'm out from under her suffocating grip I'm a little afraid to give her any power back."

"Your mom definitely isn't who I thought she was that first day I met her," Jentry laughs.

"What do you mean?"

"She's actually a pretty cool lady," Jentry smiles. "She's given me some good advice."

"When did my mom give you advice?"

"We email every once in a while," she says, shrugging like it is no big deal.

"What, you mean those inspirational emails?"

"No. Like regular emails." She takes a sip of her drink while I fight to keep my emotions in check.

"So, is she like using you to find out what I'm doing?" My hand is practically shaking with anger as I bring the coffee to my lips. How could Mom be so diabolical that she would go behind my back and use my roommate to spy on me?

In a flash, Jentry is standing in front of me, looking angrier than I've ever seen her. She wings her coffee cup toward a garbage can. The cup falls short and coffee splashes against the side of the can.

"For your information, we don't even talk about you. I needed somebody to talk to about my family stuff. And I wanted to apologize to her for making her think my mom was dead. I can't believe you think that she would do that to you. And even if she did, how could you think that I would be involved in it?"

I feel so stupid for thinking that Jentry and Mom had some spy-on-GK thing going on that I don't even know what to say. I open my mouth but nothing comes out. Jentry just stares at me with the most disappointed look on her face.

"I thought we were friends. I would never betray a friend," she says, disappearing behind a cluster of trees.

I sit on the bench for a long time, finishing my coffee, and wondering how in the world I could be so close to everything I've ever wanted, yet feeling more lost than ever. Something I've been pushing back for weeks bubbles up and I can't push it down anymore. I start sobbing into my hands. I miss my family. I don't belong here. I just want to go home.

I dial my home number again, hoping Sean doesn't answer. When I hear my mother's voice it is like eating warm chocolate cookies, snuggling by a fire, finishing the perfect book, and waking up on Christmas morning to a foot of snow all wrapped up in one moment.

"Hi, Mommy," I whisper, still crying.

"Grace Kelly, what's the matter?"

"I miss you," I admit, not caring about the gawkers walking by.

"I miss you too, sweetheart. Is there something else wrong?" she probes gently.

"Jentry is mad at me. Charlie thinks I'm a liar and now he's dating Sloane. The sisters think I'm somebody that I'm not. I was so mean to you. I don't belong here," I mumble through sobs.

"Calm down, sweetie. I don't know who Charlie and

Sloane are so I can't help with that one. But I know that Jentry is a true friend so you two will work it out. I don't know much about the sisters but I'm sure they wouldn't have picked you as a pledge if they didn't think you would belong. It's really hard for me to admit this, but you belong there. It's hard enough to leave home at eighteen, let alone sixteen. You are doing so good. Daddy and I are so proud of you."

I was expecting Mom to offer to come get me and take me away from my new, complicated life. Actually, I guess I was hoping she would. That way I could blame her for college not working out. I guess maybe I've blamed her for a lot of things I was too scared to try. If I really want to be a grown-up, I have to start acting like one all the time instead of picking and choosing the situations I want to deal with. Starting with all the lies I've told.

I'm tempted to tell Mom about the whopper of a lie I told just to get into the Alphas, but I don't.

"Grace Kelly, it wasn't right of me to keep you so sheltered all these years. I'm so sorry." I hear her choke up and my stomach clenches. I've been making her out to be such a monster for so long that I forgot she was just trying to do her best to keep me safe.

"It wasn't all you, Mom. I hid behind you a lot of times when I was too scared to make my own decisions," I admit.

"I've never wanted anything but the best for you," she says.

"Can I come home this weekend?" I beg. As bad as I want to see my family, I also want to avoid Charlie at the Monster Mash.

"You are most definitely not coming home this weekend," Mom says harshly.

"You're actually telling me that I can't come home?" I ask, amazed.

"Not after I slaved all week at my sewing machine to make a costume for you," she laughs.

"What kind of costume?" I ask, afraid to know.

"You'll see. Just make sure that you send me a picture. I'm getting pretty good at opening email attachments since Jentry explained it to me. By the way, tell her that I deleted those pictures she sent to Sean. Your brother is in a heap of trouble. I don't suppose you'll tell me what he was blackmailing you about? I couldn't get it out of Jentry."

"Gosh, Mom. I can't even remember," I lie, smiling.

"I hope that you know that you can tell me anything," she says, getting serious.

"I do, Mom," I answer, tempted to spill everything about the Alpha Bet and the lie I told about being Edwina Fay's niece to get into the sorority in the first place. But I don't. I think baby steps to the whole truth are better for now.

ELEVEN

The day of the Monster Mash is finally here. I wish I could be as excited as Jentry and the other sisters, but my stomach is in knots. I just know that Sloane will try to humiliate me by making out with Charlie right in front of me.

Jentry and I spent the morning trying to hunt down red tights to wear with her ketchup costume. Now we're back in our dorm room getting ready for the party. I'm about to slice open a package from Mom with the infamous cheerleader panty box cutter.

"Don't you dare," Jentry warns, stealing the weapon from my hand.

She slides the blade back in, then tosses is on her bed. Delicately she peels the tape off the box and pries it open.

When Mom said she made me a costume I was expecting a blue-and-white gingham Dorothy costume complete with braids, not a floor-length satin ivory gown with matching elbow gloves, a candy-cane striped sash, and fake diamond costume jewelry like Jentry just extracted out of the box. Mom also packed the satin pumps my grandma got married in, which I've coveted for years but never wore because I was too afraid I would end up in the ER. How in the world did she know that I wanted to dress up just like my favorite picture of Princess Grace of Monaco? I love that picture so much that I printed it off and taped it to my desk.

"Wait…you told her?" I ask Jentry. She is holding the dress against me, shaking her head in amazement. And to think I used to be embarrassed to wear the clothes my mom handmade for me.

"I might have mentioned it. You know, in between giving her the 411 on you giving Charlie your panties and making out with that girl," she says teasingly.

"Wow!" I gasp, spying the dress against me in the mirror.

"Your mom rocks. If you ever talk shit about her again, it's on," she jokes.

"I know," I say, actually meaning it. As much as I love the dress, it makes me even more homesick. But the fuzzy feeling knowing Mom made this especially for me to attend a fraternity party overpowers the homesickness. I can't believe how long it has taken me to realize how much my family, especially Mom, just want me to be happy. My family isn't perfect, but they're mine, and I'm lucky to have them.

Jentry lays the dress gently across my bed and moves to her desk. I can tell by the way she's moving across the room that something is wrong. Jentry is pretty good about blowing off her true feelings, but I know her change in mood has something to do with her family.

"Why don't you ever talk about your family?" I ask nervously.

"What's to talk about? My mom and dad are both workaholics who don't even care that they have a kid. The best day of their lives was the day I left for college," she says, slumping down in her desk chair.

"That can't be true. I'm sure they are just keeping themselves busy so they don't miss you so much," I say, trying to reassure her. I glance at the photograph Jentry took of her mother swinging and wonder how that woman could possibly neglect her daughter. Jentry catches me gazing at the photo.

"That's my aunt. She's the only one who has ever spent any time with me," Jentry admits.

"I'm really sorry, Jentry. I didn't know. If it's any consolation, I think they are crazy. There is nobody I'd rather spend time with than you."

"Thanks, GK. I'm sorry I dumped on you. It's just that I'd give anything to have a mom like yours," she says, working her red tights on one leg at a time.

"I'm pretty sure she'd swap you for Sean," I tease.

"I've always been afraid to trust people because of my parents," Jentry admits. "You're the first really close friend I've ever had. I knew you were different the first time I saw you."

My cheeks flame up at remembering how I accidentally

busted in on Jentry and Aaron. It seems like that all happened a million years ago. A lot has changed in ten weeks.

"I couldn't have done any of this without you," I tell her, knowing that I'll never be able to repay her.

"I don't believe that for a second, but you're welcome," she says, smiling again. "We better quit screwing around and get ready for this big party."

"Tonight is going to be hard," I admit, referring to seeing Sloane and Charlie together as a couple for the first time.

"Charlie is going to be panting when he sees you in that," Jentry laughs. I can't help but hope she's right, even though I know we can't date.

"I'm sure he'll be too busy making out with Sloane," I smart off, slipping out of my jeans. I unbutton my oxford and slip into the dress. Jentry zips it up for me and it fits like a glove. I step into my grandma's heels and arrange the sash over my dress.

"Will you quit? You don't even know for sure that they are dating. Ron said that Charlie doesn't like her," Jentry says, piling my hair in an updo. She grabs the tiara my mom put in the box and carefully slides it onto my head. I sit patiently as she applies my makeup. I don't really need her to anymore but it's kind of fun being pampered.

"Is that why they left together the other night?" I ask, unconvinced.

"I guess she told him that some guy had been following her around all night and she was scared to walk home alone. Sounds like our girl, huh?"

I can't believe I was naïve enough to fall for one of

Sloane's tricks. Why doesn't she just move on and quit trying to torture me?

"You know what sucks?" Jentry asks, stopping her eyeliner in mid-air. "She's almost done with her tasks already. God, I hate overachievers. Present company excluded, of course. She's being such a kiss-up to Lindsay because she wants to be initiated before we are."

"That's pretty funny, because Lindsay told me that there would only be one ceremony for all three of us."

"We should have wrecked her car," Jentry laughs.

"Let's not even worry about Sloane tonight," I say, even though I know that I'll be thinking of nothing else, besides Charlie, all night.

"Smile," she says, pointing her BlackBerry at me. In seconds it is on its way to my mother's email account.

"I don't know what I'd do without you," I say, pushing her cushiony condiment body through our doorway. We start giggling as we move through the hallway. To my surprise, I'm actually starting to get excited about the party. I decide to start the evening off right before we even get to the Omega house. As we pass Sloane's door I grab the marker off her board and cross out her self-professed love for Charlie. I recap her marker and throw it against the door. Then I prance out of the dorm like a true princess.

•   •   •

The Omega house is decked out in fake cobwebs, giant spiders, skeletons arranged in obscene positions, and mangled

jack-o'-lanterns. Jentry and I step very carefully over pumpkin guts strung on the front step and let ourselves in the
front door. We are greeted by vampires, witches, fairies, guys
wearing regular clothes and terrifying masks, black cats, and
one guy who is completely naked except for a tube sock over
his thing.

"That is so wrong," Jentry laughs, nearly toppling over
while pointing at the guy. I will be really happy to meet
up with Ron so that he can take responsibility for keeping
Jentry upright all night.

As if on cue, Ron waddles up looking jaundiced in
his mustard costume. They attempt to kiss each other and
nearly plow each other over.

"You two have fun now," I laugh, heading off to find
the sisters and try to spot Charlie. I can't wait to show off
my costume.

Everyone's costumes are so elaborate that I barely recognize anyone. It makes me really nervous to think that
Charlie could have already seen me without me realizing it.
I'm just about to push open the door to the kitchen when
an arm draped in black pulls me into a side hallway. I spin
around to a face full of fur.

"Jeez, April, you nearly gave me a heart attack," I say,
taking in her terrifying werewolf/vampire hybrid costume.

"Oops, sorry, Grace Kelly," she says, removing her fake
fangs. "I know this is a party and all, but I was wondering
if you would consider doing my task now?"

I suppose doing a task is one way to avoid running
into Charlie and Sloane, although I'm hardly dressed for

it. The thought of annoying Sloane by completing another task perks me up though.

"Sure, April. What do you need?"

"Every time the Omegas have a party my boyfriend disappears. I'm pretty sure he's cheating on me, but I need you to get proof."

"How am I going to do that?" I ask, praying she isn't asking me to use myself as bait.

"I'm pretty sure he'll lure somebody back to his room. I was thinking you could just sit in his closet and watch. *W* for watch," she says, weirdly unaffected by the fact that we are discussing a plan for me to spy on her boyfriend having sex with another girl.

"I have to actually watch them?" I ask, disgusted. This is really going above and beyond.

"I don't want a play-by-play. I just want to know who he's with," she clarifies. Like that is so much better.

"So I have to hide in his closet all night just hoping he'll bring a girl back?" I ask, not exactly thrilled about missing out on the entire party.

"You're right. That is pretty lame. Never mind," April says, defeated. She pops her fangs back in and starts to walk away. I grab her by the scruff of her werewolf neck.

"Hold on, I'll do it."

"Yay!" she squeals through her fangs, sending a spray of spit toward me. "Oops, sorry."

April explains that the Omega house is set up just like the Alpha house with a hidden staircase off the kitchen. At least I don't have to worry about anyone seeing me, even though I actually wanted to be seen for once. She agrees to give me ten minutes by keeping him distracted. I continue toward the kitchen area, scanning for Charlie. As bad as I don't want the awkwardness of seeing him with Sloane, I wouldn't hate it if he caught a glimpse of me in this amazing dress. I have no idea what I will even say if I find him, but I've got to at least try.

"Dang, Princess Di. You're smoking," an Omega dressed up as the Incredible Hunk says as he passes me. I smile and don't even bother to correct him.

I swing the kitchen door open to find Charlie, dressed as Fred Flintstone, manning the keg. He's staring off into space and doesn't even look up when I come into the kitchen. Two of his friends standing near him exchange looks when they see me. I smile at them as they leave the kitchen to give us some privacy. Charlie finally looks up at me. His face stays blank.

"Yabba dabba do," I say sweetly.

"Hi," he says flatly.

"Are you mad at me?" I ask, knowing this is about way more than blowing him off to answer a trivia question. God only knows what lies Sloane has filled his gorgeous head with.

"I just don't understand why you lied." He takes a giant swig of his beer and seems to sway a bit.

"Lied about what?" I ask, my palms sweating. I've told so many lies since I got to college I can't imagine which one Charlie found out about.

"You're amazing," he yells. "You put on this whole

klutzy, naïve-girl act. Meanwhile you've got everybody on campus eating out of your hand." He slams his cup of beer onto the counter and foam sloshes over the edge. He is a blur of orange and black as he storms past me out of the kitchen.

That went well. I don't have time to figure it out right now, though, because I have to get upstairs to spy on April's boyfriend.

I make my way to the back of the kitchen to find the staircase. I quietly climb the stairs and begin looking for the door that April described. It isn't hard to spot, with its door-length poster of Megan Fox. I knock lightly, just in case. When no one answers, I slip inside and close the door behind me.

It is pitch black, with the exception of a small night-light. I scan the room for the closet, finding it on the other side of the room. I start walking that direction when my heel gets caught in some clothes piled on the floor. I try to shake it loose, lose my balance, and fall right on my face in a pile of dirty clothes. And by dirty, I mean if I looked at them under a microscope I'm sure they would have an entire germ subdivision living on them. At least they broke my fall.

I'm trying to untangle myself when I hear someone whistling out in the hallway. I scramble to my feet and make my way to the closet. I'm pulling the rickety door open when I hear the doorknob turn. I crouch down in the bottom of the closet and pull the door closed behind me.

"Home sweet home," I hear a male voice say. I can

barely hear anything over the roar of my own heart beating in my ears. If this guy doesn't bust me in his closet it will be a miracle. Charlie would really think I'm a freak if one of his frat brothers found me hiding in his closet. I close my eyes and hope that I can pull this off.

I hear April's boyfriend rattling around in his room, whispering things every now and then, but I can't quite catch what he is saying. Not that I really want to. I sit very still and try hard not to peek out of the slats in the closet doors.

"Finally," he says, sighing deeply. I hear what sounds like clothing dropping to the floor. I try to block out the image of a half-naked girl standing in the middle of his bedroom. I hear him plop down on the bed, messing around with something.

It is quiet for a few minutes and I'm thinking I lucked out and they are just going to take a nap or something.

"Sweet! Score!" he yells, making me bang my head against the back of the closet. Luckily it only makes a loud noise inside my head. I'm tempted to peek because I haven't heard another person yet, but on second thought, I don't really want to see him going at it solo either.

Maybe I'll just tell April I looked. But she did say that she wanted to know who he was with. I guess I could lie and say they still had their costumes on. That wouldn't be very sisterly though. I think I hear some grunting and I immediately have the urge to throw up in one of April's boyfriend's shoes. I just have to look really quick then squeeze my eyes closed again. I push myself up to one of the slats in the door and peer out.

I almost fall through the closet door laughing at what I see. April's boyfriend is sitting alone on his bed in his underwear, his Superman costume pooled at his ankles, playing some kind of boxing video game. He has a controller in one hand and a punching glove on the other and is egging on the opponent like he's standing right in front of him. So this is who he is cheating on April with. She's going to get a kick out of this.

"David, are you in there?" April's voice says from in the hall. She bangs on the door, causing David to jump off the bed, turn off the video game, and slip back into his Superman costume. He waits for her to go back downstairs before sneaking out.

I pull myself out of the closet and head downstairs to give April the good news. I slip past a vampire couple making out in a corner of the kitchen. A costume contest is starting and people are arranged in groups according to gender and year of college. Cheers erupt as the winners are announced. I cheer the loudest when Ron and Jentry win best couple. They look adorable trying to hug each other while jointly holding their trophy.

"Who is she?" April storms up, definitely not as laid back about the possibility of her boyfriend cheating as she was earlier.

"You are not going to believe this," I say. "I was really afraid to look out—"

"Just tell me who the bitch is," April says viciously. I take a step back.

"He isn't cheating on you, April. He was playing video games the whole time."

Her face, contorted with anger, slowly begins to return to normal.

"He didn't have a girl with him?" she asks, amazed.

"Nope. Maybe he just doesn't like the party scene," I suggest.

"Yeah, he's always saying he would rather it just be the two of us."

"He seems like a good guy. You just might want to mention that he should keep up a little better on his laundry," I laugh.

"Thanks, Grace Kelly. You're the best," she says, hugging me, then tearing through the crowd to find her Clark Kent.

I make my way over to where some of the sisters are listening to the winners of the costume contest. They're dressed like the Pussycat Dolls and I can almost hear their brains whirring trying to figure out who I am dressed like.

"Princess Di," I respond, saving myself the trouble of explaining who Princess Grace is. They ooh and ahh at my tiara before turning their attention back to the winners.

The sisters and I are still laughing about the sock costume guy who just walked by when I notice people start to stare at me. I get the feeling it has nothing to do with me not winning the costume contest.

The weight of their stares bears down on me. I notice

that several of them are holding white pieces of paper. I watch their eyes glance down at the paper, then back at me. Within seconds the scrutiny is over as most of them ball up the papers and toss them around the room. They go right back to dancing and talking and I almost wonder if I imagined the whole thing. Just as I am about to reach down and get a balled-up paper, I lock eyes with Sloane. She is standing alone in a corner of the room dressed in a skintight red bodysuit, red stilettos, and red horns protruding from her perfect blonde locks. I drop my eyes immediately, fearful that her eyes might singe my soul. I squat down and grab a wadded ball of paper. I straighten up and smooth it out. A blown-up picture of my state identification card with the words, "Not Legal to Drive" glares up at me. My birth date is circled in black marker just in case someone would dare miss it. This cannot be happening.

I knew that Sloane was out to get me, like taking Charlie wasn't bad enough. Now she has to humiliate me in front of all my sorority sisters. At least Lindsay already knows so I probably won't get in any trouble. But the sisters might feel that I completely betrayed them by lying. I really wanted to be able to tell them myself when I was ready.

I steady myself and glance around. The party hasn't skipped a beat. No one is staring angrily at me. No one cares. The papers are discarded all over the floor, just like empty beer cups. Sloane tried her best to humiliate me and nobody is even paying attention. I look back at her, feeling stronger now, meeting the fire in her eyes. Is this really still about a little bit of marinara sauce on her dress? She stomps out of the room, and a few seconds later, I hear the front door slam shut.

I'm so overjoyed that I beat Sloane that I practically want to do cartwheels across the room. I remember very quickly the shoes I have on, not to mention the dress. It doesn't stop my insides from doing cartwheels of joy. My happiness dissipates quickly when I notice Charlie by a window looking at one of the papers. He shakes his head in disgust. Sloane must have told him about my age and that is why he accused me of lying. I weave my way through the crowd to him.

"I can explain," I say when I'm close enough to touch him.

"I'm not interested," Charlie says, lifting his glass to his lips.

"I didn't lie to you. I just didn't volunteer the information," I defend myself. "When I realized you could get in trouble for dating me, that's when I backed off."

"You can spin it however you want, Grace Kelly. But you're still a liar." He won't even look at me.

"Look around. Nobody even cares," I say, gesturing to the other Greeks dancing and socializing around us.

"I don't give a crap about your age, Grace Kelly. Although it does explain how immature you've been acting," he says disgustedly. His comment practically makes me clutch my chest in pain. I thought I had been acting so mature and sophisticated.

"Have you told so many lies that you can't even keep

them straight?" he asks me when I don't respond. The fake black eyebrows he's wearing are in a taut line across his forehead. I wouldn't have thought fun-loving Charlie to be capable of such anger. I wish I could at least figure out why he is mad at me. I can only imagine the lies that Sloane told him about me.

"Grace Kelly, look at us," my fellow sisters, Eve and Amber giggle excitedly, interrupting us. They're both dressed identically as Edwina Fay. I glance up at Charlie, suddenly remembering that other huge lie I told.

TWELVE

Eve and Amber scamper off as quickly as they came, leaving the air between Charlie and me rigid with tension. He can't know. How could he know? The only way he could know that I lied about Edwina Fay being my aunt is if Sloane somehow found out. If Sloane knew she would have already told the sisters and I would have been kicked to the curb already.

"Tell the truth, Grace Kelly," he urges. His eyes beg me to come clean, but I've been lying so long that I just can't. I can't risk losing the Alphas if by some small chance Charlie doesn't know the truth.

"I don't know what you're talking about," I lie, looking away from him.

The party rages around us but it feels like we are in our own personal vortex. Charlie crushes his empty plastic cup in his hand and angrily tosses it away.

"You do know what I'm talking about. If you want to be with me then I need to hear you say it," he says desperately.

"Be with you?" I shout. "I'm pretty sure the position of girlfriend is already taken. Talk about someone being dishonest," I bluff. I know that Ron told Jentry that Charlie didn't like Sloane, but maybe he was lying.

"What are you talking about?" he asks, confused.

"Does the name Sloane Masterson ring a bell?" I smart off.

Charlie's fake eyebrows crinkle up and I have to hand it to him. He actually looks like he has no idea what I'm talking about.

"You mean that girl I'm planning the Jingle Bell Run with?" he asks.

He almost had me. I almost believed that he cared about me. But I can't ignore the fact that he just lied right to my face. Not like I'm any better, but at least my lies don't have anything to do with Charlie. He is obviously trying to play me, Sloane, and who knows how many other girls. I know for a fact that the Alphas aren't participating in the Jingle Bell Run this year. Charlie is just as big of a liar as I am.

"Leave me alone," I say, turning to walk away. Charlie grabs my arm and pulls me to him. I hate that I still have such a strong urge to kiss his pillowy-soft lips.

"Tell me the truth about Edwina Fay," he says, loosening his grip on my arm but not letting go. I hear myself gasp.

"She's my aunt?" I answer, but it comes out sounding

like a question. Charlie obviously knows the truth some-how, but I still can't bring myself to admit it.

"No, she isn't," he says, looking distraught.

"How do you know?" I ask indignantly. I figure I'm going down in flames either way, so I might as well do it in style.

"Because she's mine." He lets go of my arm and storms out of the Omega house, leaving me gaping after him in a very un-princess-like way.

• • •

Hours, days, then weeks pass, just waiting for my world to crumble. I know any day now Charlie will tell Lindsay and the other sisters that I lied about being a legacy. After today, I only have four tasks left. Lindsay is already plan-ning Sloane's, Jentry's, and my initiation ceremony for the day we get back from Thanksgiving break, which is only eight days away. I know that the sisters should hear the truth from me, but I'm just so close to being a full-blown sister. The least I can do is finish out my tasks.

I trudge across campus, dressed all in black. I push all thoughts of being kicked out of the sorority out of my head. I have to be sharp for these three tasks. The likeli-hood of being initiated at this point seems as likely as life on Mars, but I still want to complete all my tasks to show the sisters that completing the tasks and becoming one of them was important to me.

I slip into the Omega house undetected to complete

tasks *J*, *O*, and *R*. I'm almost more familiar with this house than I am my own. The active sisters all came together last night for an emergency meeting after hearing a terrifying rumor. I only know this because I was informed by text message this morning that I should raid the Omega house to steal back our panties, just in time (*J*, *O*, *R*). If I hadn't heard the rumor last night about the Omegas planning to raffle off our panties for the Greek auction, I wouldn't understand what all the fuss was about. But there is no way I'm letting random perverts bid on my silky pink panties.

Apparently the guys aren't too concerned with cleanliness, because I'm pretty sure some of the garbage on the floor is left over from their party almost three weeks ago. Gross. Unfortunately not all of the Omegas have the same commitment to education as Charlie, so one of the sisters had to place an anonymous phone call to the house inviting them to the grand opening of a new donut shop where the servers are all dressed in bikinis. She gave them the address of a vacant building across town and told them they should wait in their cars and when the shop opened, the girls would roller skate out to take their orders. When I saw them piling into their cars, still hung over, I almost felt sorry for them. Then I remembered they were about to put my unmentionables on the auction block.

I tiptoe up the back stairs and search frantically for a pile of underwear. I see bras and panties here and there, but I'm pretty sure those are just from random hookups. Double gross.

I'm not having any luck and I try to think: if I were an

oversexed, beer drinking, average-intelligence guy, where would I put my most valuable possession? It might sound a little extreme, but the Greek auction is the most competitive Greek competition of the year. All the sororities and fraternities compete to see who can make the most money by auctioning off random items. Then all of the money goes to local charities. It's one of those everybody-wins kind of situations. Except being the biggest moneymaker entitles you to bragging rights for the entire year.

I don't even notice the glass trophy case against the wall until my foot gets snagged on the corner of it. It throws me forward and I slam into a closed bedroom door. I spin around, fearing the entire trophy case is about to land on my head, but there isn't so much as a trophy wobbling. I wipe invisible sweat off my brow in relief. I'm about to search another bedroom when a silky white Victoria's Secret tag, hanging off the edge of a giant, gold metal cup trophy, catches my eye in the mirrored back of the case. It would have been the perfect hiding spot if it weren't for the errant tag.

The trophy case has a sliding door on each end and is locked by a simple key lock. Not exactly Fort Knox, but I'm not trained on breaking and entering either. I survey the case, trying to think of a way to get it without smashing the whole thing to smithereens with an ax. That wouldn't exactly be subtle. The Alphas want the Omegas clueless about the raid for as long as possible so they don't have time to find something else good to auction off. I spin my Alpha pin on my collar in frustration, trying to figure out a way to get in the case.

I go from room to room looking for something that could be used to try and pry one of the doors open enough to reach my hand in. When I open Charlie's door I can smell him. It is a symphony for my olfactory senses. I'm nearly giddy when I spot a metal letter opener on his desk. I go to grab it but stop when I spot my panties in a plastic baggy on the corner of his desk. Written on them in black Sharpie is "Grace Kelly, not for sale." My heart nearly bursts with joy.

I grab the letter opener and jam it in the lock. It turns as smoothly as if it were the key. The Omegas seriously need to consider investing in better security. I shove my hand into the trophy cup and pull out all the sisters' underwear. I jam the huge bunches into my pockets, relock the trophy case, and put back Charlie's letter opener. I leave the baggy on his desk, knowing the contents are in good hands.

"I can't believe you woke me up for that," an angry voice booms from downstairs. The front door slams and I hear several grunts of agreement.

I try not to freak out when I realize that I'm trapped on the second floor of the Omega house with pocketfuls of girl panties, dressed like a cat burglar. I don't want to know what Charlie would do if he found me in the house. I've only seen him in passing on campus lately and he always looks past me like he doesn't even see me. The only way anyone would believe I belonged here is if I was naked and asleep in one of the beds. I consider that option, but only for a second. Then I quietly open Charlie's window, pop out the screen, and shimmy out onto the trellis climbing the length of the house.

This would be a bad situation for a normal person, but for someone with my accident-prone injury record, it's surely going to result in a full-body cast. I guess I can look at the bright side; I won't have to admit to the sisters that I lied about being Edwina Fay's legacy. I can just imagine the laugh Sloane will get out of this. What are the odds that I would lie about being the niece of the aunt of a guy I am totally crushing on? I'll have plenty of time to run the numbers when I'm not a Greek anymore. I lower myself down the trellis slowly and carefully.

Suddenly my foot slips, and I'm hanging onto the trellis for dear life trying to get my foothold again. But the vines growing on the trellis are slick with morning dew and I can't get leverage. The trellis pulls loose from the house, and for a second I'm mid-air, dangling from a flimsy piece of vinyl. I try to calculate my distance from the ground and my likelihood of survival, but the trellis flips back too fast. Before I can compute anything, I'm sprawled out in a huge pile of leaves with the trellis on top of me.

"I'm alive," I tell no one and push the trellis off me. I cover myself up with leaves and play possum for a minute in case the ruckus gets the attention of the guys. After a few minutes I realize they are still too busy licking their wounds over the non-existent donut shop to care about their frat house falling apart. I bolt out of the leaves and down the street to the Alpha house.

• • •

"What happened to you?" Lindsay asks, trying hard not to laugh. I sneak a glance in the mirror hanging in the foyer of the Alpha house. My hair looks like a rat's nest with leaves sticking out of it at all angles. I have a big scratch on my left cheek and something black on my right eyelid.

"You should see the other guy," I joke, wondering how long it will take the Omegas to notice the broken trellis in their front yard.

"You did great, Grace Kelly," Lindsay says, holding out a plastic bag for me to empty my pockets into. "You're almost done. There isn't much standing in the way of you becoming a real sister now," she says, sounding relieved. She pulls down the *J*, *O*, and *R* and crumples them up. I gaze up at the *E*, *F*, *L*, and *T* remaining. *E* and *F* will be done if I can just bribe Amber and Eve with a big box of Edwina Fay cosmetics instead of a visit like they have been begging for.

"There is nothing I want more than to be an Alpha," I tell her. I know I should come clean about my lie and just get it over with, but I can't seem to bring myself to tell Lindsay the truth.

"Our sorority is special. Not all sororities have the bond that Alpha girls have. Your aunt made sure of that. She was a visionary when she created a sorority that focused on picking girls who would enhance each other's lives. She took a stance against hazing and inter-sorority competitiveness. It would be really great if you could get her to visit for the Greek auction. We'd win for sure," Lindsay says, her eyes glazed over a bit. Oh, sure. I'll just dial up the CEO of the most powerful cosmetics company in the world and invite her over.

I can't do this anymore. Lindsay has been so nice to me from the very beginning and I've just been lying to her face. How can I even think about calling myself a true sister?

"Lindsay, there's something I need to tell you," I say, spinning my Alpha pin one last time.

"Sure, Grace Kelly. You can tell me anything," Lindsay says, guiding me over to a loveseat.

My eyes start watering immediately at the thought of never being allowed back into this beautiful house. I take a couple of deep breaths and push back the tears.

"I haven't been completely honest with you," I start out. Lindsay cocks her head to the side in surprise.

"Is this about your age again?" she asks. I wish that was all this was about.

"Not exactly. Do you remember the night of rush? When I came back to tell you that I was a legacy? That Edwina Fay was my aunt?" I drag out.

"Uh-huh," Lindsay says.

"Well, I wasn't really telling the full truth," I admit, ready to collapse in a heap onto the floor.

"Which part did you lie about?" Lindsay asks, confused.

"The whole—"

"GK, there you are," Jentry says, busting into the room. "I've been looking everywhere for you," she bluffs, giving me a look that tells me she just heard everything.

"No offense, Jentry, but Grace Kelly was just in the middle of telling me something really important," Lindsay says, trying to shoo Jentry away.

"Oh, Grace Kelly, I keep telling you that you don't need to keep feeling guilty about practically being Alpha royalty. I'm sure Lindsay will understand that you didn't come clean about being a legacy in the first place because you wanted to get into the sorority on your own merits."

"Is that what this is about?" Lindsay says, placing a hand on my knee. Jentry bores her eyes into mine, daring me to disagree.

"Um, kind of. I wanted the Alphas to want me for me," I answer. At least it isn't a lie.

"Don't be silly, we all love you here. The only reason you weren't on our list was because National capped new enrollment at two pledges, but luckily they made an exception for legacies."

"I keep telling her to quit worrying," Jentry says, dragging me off the loveseat.

"Just think, Grace Kelly. In just a few days, you'll be going through your initiation ceremony and then you'll be an official Alpha."

"I can't wait," I tell her as Jentry drags me out the front door.

"What were you about to do?" Jentry asks, after we get far enough away from the Alpha house that there is no chance of anyone hearing us.

"Tell the truth. Finally," I admit.

"Are you insane? You are this close to getting everything

you want," she says, gesturing with her thumb and index finger.

I hadn't confided in Jentry about Charlie knowing the truth. As hard as it was to keep it from her, I knew that she would be as disappointed as I am. I didn't want to crush her like that, but now I see that I should tell her the truth.

I gesture for her to take a seat on a bench in the quad. I sit down next to her, wishing I had more than a sweatshirt on to fight the brisk November air.

"Do you remember the night of the Monster Mash?"

"Sort of. That punch the Omegas served was wicked good," she laughs.

"I found out that night that Charlie knows I lied about being Edwina Fay's niece."

She gasps and holds a hand to her mouth. "How?"

"He knew I had lied because she is his aunt," I reveal.

"SHUT UP!" Jentry screams, burying her face in her hands.

"I know. Talk about your rotten luck. I need to do the right thing and tell the sisters the truth."

"But he hasn't told yet and that was three weeks ago," Jentry says brightly.

I realize for the first time that my lies haven't only hurt me. They've hurt all the people I care about, the people I want to care about me. They are going to suffer because I chose to lie.

"It's time for me to grow up," I say, knowing that no matter how much I tried to convince myself I was acting mature, I haven't been.

"But we're going to be initiated soon," Jentry pleads.

"That will just make it worse. Besides, I don't want to embarrass the sorority like that."

"Can you just wait until tomorrow?" Jentry whispers, pulling her legs into her chest and rocking back and forth on the bench.

She's so upset that I can't help but agree. I want to clear things up with Charlie first anyway, so he knows that I'm going to finally tell the truth. In less than twenty-four hours, I won't be an Alpha anymore.

• • •

"Don't think I'm done with you," Sloane growls as I pass by her room, soaking wet, having just come from the shower. I figured showing up at the Omega house with dirt on my face and leaves in my hair might be a dead giveaway that I had stolen the panties.

"You are the only thing about the Alphas that I'm not going to miss," I say, too quietly for Sloane to hear me. I can only hope that when I leave the Alphas, Sloane will give up her personal mission to destroy me.

I slip back into my empty dorm room to get dressed. Jentry got a phone call from Eve telling her to get to the Alpha house right away. I thought it was kind of strange that I didn't get a call, but I guess I better start getting used to it.

I decide on jeans and a McMillan College sweatshirt with my hair pulled up in a ponytail and no makeup. I leave my Alpha pin lying on the dresser inside my closet. I'm coming back to the room after I talk to Charlie, to get all of my Alpha mementos to return when I tell them the truth.

I'm waiting for the elevator when I notice a neon green poster reminding students that the deadline to submit their entries for the science fair is the last night of Thanksgiving break. How could I have forgotten? How will it look if last year's winner doesn't submit an entry? And not just any entry, but something mind-blowing.

The stress of everything is too much. My mom was right. I am completely overwhelmed. I just want to hide out in my parents' house and never come out. I know that wouldn't solve anything and is completely immature, but I don't even care.

The elevator doors ding and open. Blurry-eyed, I start walking into it and run into someone.

"Oh, I'm really sorry," I say, looking up into Charlie's face.

"Just the girl I was looking for," he says, guiding me back out of the elevator, into the lounge.

• • •

Neither of us says a word as we settle into an overstuffed couch.

"I was just coming to find you," I tell him.

"Me first," he insists. "I should never have spoken to you like that. I'm so sorry," he says, taking my hand and rubbing it against his face. Touching him feels amazing, especially since I never thought I would get to do it again. "I don't care that you lied."

"I do. I'm so sorry that I dragged your family into this," I say, embarrassed.

"Are you kidding? My aunt would be flattered," he laughs.

"It was wrong and I'm going to fix it tonight." I feel bad going back on what I told Jentry, but I have to come clean to the Alphas tonight.

"One mistake doesn't make you a bad person, Grace Kelly."

I wish I could believe him.

"You do what you have to do, but don't do it because of me. I'm not going to say a word," he promises, zipping his mouth shut with an imaginary zipper.

"It's time. I would rather the sisters find out the truth from me." My decision is made and I don't even feel nervous about it anymore.

"I don't really care if you're an Alpha. I just want to be with you," Charlie says, making me glad I'm sitting down because I probably would have collapsed. "If you need me after you tell the Alphas, I'll be at the Omega house," he says, leaning over to kiss my cheek. He gets onto the open elevator, looking back once to wink at me. I lean back into the couch cushions, nearly giddy.

Suddenly, I feel someone watching me. I turn to see Sloane at the entrance of our hallway, fire blazing in her eyes. In all my excitement over Charlie forgiving me for lying, I had forgotten all about him lying to me.

THIRTEEN

I don't have the energy to even think about what is going on between Charlie and Sloane right now. I have to get to the Alpha house and finally tell them the truth. I make my way, slowly, back to my dorm room. I don't think I have ever dreaded anything as much as I dread telling the sisters that I lied to get into their sorority. I'm not stupid enough to think that they will let me stay in the sorority. I just hope, in time, they can somehow forgive me.

My phone rings in my pocket right as I'm turning the door handle to my room. I pull it out of my pocket to see Jentry's name on the screen. I slip it back into my pocket, unanswered, because I know she will just try and talk me out of what I'm about to do. And it wouldn't take much convincing for me to keep lying. I have to make this right.

I load up my messenger bag with all my picture frames, T-shirts, and other Alpha paraphernalia. I'm sure the Alphas won't want me keeping any of it. I attach my pledge pin to my sweatshirt, knowing that the next time I touch it, I'll be taking it off for good.

I check my reflection in the mirror. I look almost as pathetic as I feel. I'm locking the door when my phone rings again. It's Jentry. The girl is nothing if not persistent. I ignore it again, already feeling my resolve weaken. I shake it off and head out of the door toward the Alpha house.

My heart is beating in overdrive as I make my way across campus. I know I should be shivering in nothing but a sweatshirt to protect me from the bitter November air, but my adrenaline is flowing so fast that I don't even feel the cold wind.

I can make out the battery-operated candles that Lindsay just put in all of the Alpha windows. I'm supposed to help her decorate the house for the holidays tomorrow so everything is up when we return from Thanksgiving break. I guess she'll have to recruit someone else now because after tonight, I will never be welcome in this house again. I walk up to the giant front door and grasp the gold handle. I can't bring myself to squeeze it to let myself in. I have to sear this last moment of being an Alpha into my mind.

My phone rings again, breaking my concentration. This time it's Charlie and I can't even begin to deal with that situation on top of this one, so I let it roll to voicemail. I squeeze the handle and let myself into the Alpha house for the last time.

It is oddly quiet when I walk into the foyer. Usually the house is filled with laughter coming from all areas of the house. I can't help but feel the ominous vibe has something to do with my lie. I secure my messenger bag on my shoulder and head toward the great room. I stop dead in my tracks when I see every single one of the sisters gathered there.

"We were beginning to think you'd abandoned us," Lindsay jokes, coming up beside me to usher me into the room. I try to gauge the expressions of the girls. Did they find out the truth? Are they all waiting here to inflict some terrible retribution on me? My stomach starts to roll until I realize that the girls actually look happy to see me. Excited almost. Some of them seem ready to bounce right out of their chairs. This isn't the behavior I would expect from girls who have found out they have been lied to for almost three months. Which makes what I have to do even harder.

"What's going on?" I ask, locking eyes with Jentry. The look she gives me nearly brings me to my knees. Something is very wrong.

"Girls," Lindsay says, gesturing to Eve and Amber who are standing at the other entrance to the room, looking like they are about to pee in their pants.

"Okay, so we wanted to surprise you because you only have three tasks left and you've been such an awesome pledge," Eve begins.

"Actually, she only has one task left now," Amber says, confusing me.

"Oh, right," Eve agrees. "We wanted to do something really special. So … ," she draws out, nearly killing me with suspense. Just when I think I can't handle the pressure of not knowing what is happening anymore, a loud crashing noise comes from the foyer and Charlie comes bounding into the great room looking flushed.

"Grace Kelly," he forces out, panting hard. Charlie is a seasoned runner so I know he must have run from pretty far away to tell me something very important. He looks at the sisters, then leans down to whisper in my ear. Eve acts like she doesn't see him and continues.

"We invited your aunt to the house," she screams, jumping up and down. I look to Charlie, then Jentry, with utter desperation as Edwina Fay herself strolls into the great room.

"So, you're my niece, huh?" she says, staring me down in front of everyone. My messenger bag slides off my shoulder and crashes to the ground, destroying the picture frame inside. Sort of like my life.

My first thought is that Edwina Fay is much prettier in person. My second i s that Charlie looks a lot like her. My third is that my entire life just combusted. I'm too stunned to even speak. Edwina hugs Charlie while keeping a close eye on me. After Charlie pulls out of his aunt's hug, he drapes his arm supportively around me, which I appreciate, since I feel that I could crumble into pieces any minute.

"Grace Kelly, what's going on?" Lindsay finally asks.

This is it. It's really over. The minute I admit to what I've done, I go back to being geeky Grace Kelly who spends her Friday nights studying. But at least that girl wasn't lying to anyone. I'm more embarrassed about who I've become than I ever was of that geeky girl who liked to study so much.

"*L* is for liar," I begin. I guess tasks *E* and *F* are complete now that Edwina Fay is here. That just leaves *T*, not that I'll get a chance to complete my tasks now. "I'm not really a legacy. I don't even know Edwina Fay. I didn't mean to hurt anyone; I just wanted in the Alpha house so badly."

I thought the sisters would scream and yell at me when they found out they had been betrayed, but no one says a word. Jentry has silent tears rolling down her face. Lindsay looks like someone knocked the wind right out of her. The rest of the sisters just keep looking back and forth at each other like someone is going to tell them this is all a big joke. Sloane stands in a back corner smirking. I can't imagine how thrilled she must be. She didn't even have to destroy me; I did that all on my own.

"I don't understand," Lindsay says, coming closer to me. "I verified your status with National."

"I called and pretended to be Edwina Fay," I lie. I hate to keep lying, but there is no way I'm ratting Jentry out for doing me a favor. Edwina Fay raises her eyebrows, obviously disturbed by my level of deceit.

"The truth is, I just wanted to find a place I felt comfortable. I've never really felt comfortable in my own skin, but I did when I was with all of you." I look around to each and every sister, avoiding Sloane. Every pair of eyes is filled with disappointment. "I'm so sorry," I say, looking at Edwina Fay. She gives me a tiny smile filled with pity and nods her forgiveness. I bend down to grab my messenger bag and hold it out to Lindsay. She takes it tentatively, obviously still stunned. I pluck my Alpha pin off my collar and hold it out to her. She hesitates, then gently takes it from me. I leave the Alpha house for the very last time.

• • •

I cry until my tear ducts are completely empty. Okay, that actually isn't humanly possible unless you are on the brink of death from dehydration, which is how I feel, although obviously I'm not. Just two weeks ago I was shopping for an initiation dress with Jentry and now I'm all alone on the fourth floor of the library surrounded by dusty old books. I needed to find a safe place and this is the only place I could think of.

I feel a little bit like Pluto. One day things are going along fine and you're still a planet, then, WHAM! Somebody decides you aren't. Okay, so maybe my situation isn't completely similar, but being stripped of my Alpha status sure feels like it.

"Here you are," Charlie says, startling me.

"What are you doing here?" I ask, wiping furiously at my damp cheeks.

"I wanted to make sure you were alright. That must have been tough."

I just shrug my shoulders and try to brush off the scene that just played out at the Alpha house like it was any other normal night.

"They aren't mad at you," Charlie insists, taking hold of one of my hands.

"Yeah, that's what Henry the VIII's second wife thought, too," I add.

"Seriously. They're just confused. You didn't have to lie, you know. They would have picked you anyway." Charlie runs his other hand across my jaw line and it feels so good that for a second I forget to feel guilty that I dragged him and his family into my desperate attempt at acceptance.

I close my eyes and focus solely on Charlie's touch. Maybe things won't be so bad. I mean, Jentry is still my best friend. My classes are going great. My relationship with my mom has never been better. And best of all, I still have Charlie. Wait.

I jerk away from Charlie's touch like he scalded me. "We can't be together," I say, suddenly remembering that my age could get him into big trouble.

"Says who?" he asks, looking amused.

"Um, the law," I respond, rolling my eyes.

"You aren't the only person who graduated high school early, you know," he says teasingly.

"What? You?" I ask, shocked.

"I started here last year when I was only sixteen. I just turned seventeen over the summer. We don't have to worry about the age thing for a while," he reassures me.

If I had any tears left I would probably cry, knowing how long I tortured myself to stay away from Charlie so that I wouldn't get him into trouble.

"It's going to be alright," Charlie tells me, moving

closer. Before I can respond, his lips are on mine, making me believe every word.

• • •

An hour later, I'm sitting cross-legged on my bed waiting for Jentry to come home. Making out with Charlie calmed my nerves for a while but as soon as I got back to our room, I wanted to know what was happening at the Alpha house. I didn't dare try to call Jentry while she was with the sisters. I'm already afraid that she may be in trouble by association.

I bolt off my bed when I hear her key in the lock. I yank the door open and nearly scare her half to death.

"I'm pissed at you," she says, breezing past me. I take my time shutting and locking the door, almost afraid to turn around and hear what she has to say. Losing the Alphas is hard enough, but losing Jentry would be unspeakable.

"I called you so many times to warn you," she yells, kicking the bag of clothes I have packed for Thanksgiving break. My parents are supposed to be coming to get me tomorrow but I'm tempted to make my way to the bus station tonight.

"They would have found out anyway," I tell her, avoiding her eyes.

"Why didn't you tell them that I'm the one who pretended to be Edwina Fay on the phone?" she screams. I look at her and see tears streaking down her cheeks. I feel like someone used my stomach to practice karate chops on. I hurt the sisters, Charlie, Edwina Fay, and worst of all, Jentry. The one person who was there for me as Grace Kelly or GK.

"I'm really sorry," I whisper, knowing it will never be enough.

"I'm quitting," she offers half-heartedly.

"No, you aren't, and I wouldn't want you to." I'm not dumb enough to believe that the dynamic between Jentry and me won't change with her being an Alpha and me not, but I would never allow her to sacrifice her happiness because of my bad judgment.

"You're the best friend I've ever had, Grace Kelly," she says, looking embarrassed.

It is the nicest thing that anyone has ever said to me. Maybe things don't have to change. I'm in lots of other activities that Jentry isn't in, like the Science Club. Which reminds me that I only have Thanksgiving break to come up with a kick-butt idea to submit for the science fair. I'm going to be just as busy as Jentry, but we'll make time for each other. We don't have to grow apart. Besides, it isn't the quantity of time we spend together but the quality.

"We're more than friends, Jentry. We're sisters. How about spending Thanksgiving with me and my family?" I ask, realizing that Jentry hasn't mentioned going home for the holiday and none of her bags are packed.

"I couldn't do that," she says shyly.

"My mom makes the best turkey and mashed potatoes in the world. I know they would love to see you, especially Sean," I wink at her.

"Really?"

"Get your stuff packed. Let's get out of here."

• • •

Two hours later, we're stuffed on a bus with other students and random strangers making our way home. I can't believe I'm actually relieved to be heading home, but after the devastation of tonight I'm ready to be hovered over for a few days. I sneak a glance at Jentry, who looks positively giddy. I wonder if this is the only real holiday she has ever had. I can't help but feel sorry for her family, for not recognizing how special she is. I realize that until a few weeks ago, I felt the same way about my mom.

"Does your mom make sweet potatoes with those tiny marshmallows on top?" Jentry asks, all giggly.

"Those are Sean's favorite. It'll be fun to watch him try not to fight you for them," I laugh.

"Do you guys all go around the table and say what you are thankful for?"

"Are you spying on us?"

She claps her hands together with glee, our holiday obviously coming close to perfection in her mind.

"We'll see how great you think it is when you have to wear a homemade Pilgrim hat," I tell her.

We're quiet for a few minutes, watching the campus disappear behind us. Jentry clears her throat and seems to want to tell me something. I've been dying to ask her what happened after I left the Alpha house earlier, but it didn't seem right to put her on the spot like that.

"They aren't mad, you know," she says, reaffirming Charlie's thoughts. "Just hurt."

"It was an immature thing to do. I knew that eventually it would blow up in my face. I'm just sorry that so many other people got hurt."

"I should never have called National. Then it would have ended that first day," Jentry says, sounding guilty.

"That's the nicest thing anyone has ever done for me. You knew how bad I wanted to be an Alpha."

"I had my own agenda though," she says, shaking her head.

"It's over, Jentry. It was fun while it lasted."

"I'm really sorry, GK."

"I'm fine. I've still got you, my classes, my family, and Charlie."

She raises her eyebrows when I mention Charlie's name. She looks about to warn me off of him when I hold my hands out in front of me.

"He's only seventeen, Jentry. He started college at sixteen just like I did. Isn't that amazing?" I squeal.

"Yeah, but Grace Kelly—"

"It will get a bit tricky next year when he turns eighteen and I'm only seventeen, but by then we can prove we have been in a relationship for a year."

"But, Grace Kelly—"

"I know, I know. I might have to skip the family

reunions for a while until his family forgives me for dragging them into my mess," I tell her.

"But, Grace Kelly. What about Charlie and Sloane?"

One time Sean threw a container full of ice-cold water on me while I was in the shower. I feel the same way right now. I was so excited that Charlie and I could be together that I didn't remember why we shouldn't be. With everything else going on, I had completely forgotten about his relationship with Sloane. How could I have been so naïve?

• • •

Fifty miles later, I'm still smacking my forehead over the fact that I forgot Charlie bold-faced lied to me.

"Maybe he just got confused," Jentry says, sticking up for him.

"No, he specifically said they were just planning the Jingle Bell Run together, and I heard Lindsay telling some active sisters that the Alphas aren't going to participate this year because of the Zetas."

"Okay, so he's a liar," Jentry agrees, shrugging her shoulders. "Sorry, GK."

"No biggie," I lie, feeling like the biggest idiot in the world for making out with Charlie in the library earlier tonight. "I'm telling him off when I get back to school," I say, my embarrassment quickly turning to anger.

"Look, there's your family," Jentry shouts excitedly as the bus pulls up to the terminal. I turn to look out the window and when I see my whole family, wearing Pilgrim hats, waving frantically at us, I forget all about Charlie.

· · ·

"If you feed me any more, I'm going to make you sew elastic into all my pants," Jentry jokes, digging into another piece of Mom's pumpkin pie. This has been the best Thanksgiving ever. We've done nothing but eat, play games, and watch movies all day. I didn't have to worry about putting on makeup, doing my hair, or even getting out of my pajamas.

"Dinner was really great, Mom," I say. Mom beams with pride and I wonder why it took me so long to realize how hard she has to work to make our lives run so smoothly. She winks at me. Sean tips the nozzle of the aerosol can of whipped topping into his mouth and fills it up. We all crack up watching him trying to swallow the puffy cream before it squishes out of his mouth. My dad pulls his shirt out of his pants and I know if Jentry weren't here, he would be unbuttoning them too.

"You are the master of turkey, darling," he says laughing.

Sean and Dad disappear into the living room to watch football while Mom, Jentry, and I stay at the dining room table to talk.

"I'm not in the sorority anymore," I blurt out. It has been killing me not to tell Mom about the Alphas and I just can't keep it in anymore.

"What happened?" Mom asks, concerned. Jentry excuses

herself, knowing I need some time alone to tell Mom the truth.

"I only got in because I lied. I told them I was the niece of a previous member so that they would have to make me a pledge," I admit.

"That's not like you, Grace Kelly," Mom says, shocked.

"Believe me, I'm not proud of it. The worst part of all is that I let the sisters down. They were all so nice to me and I just kept lying to them."

"Everybody makes mistakes. Maybe they just need some time to process everything," Mom consoles me.

"It doesn't work like that, Mom. I'm not an Alpha anymore." It's the first time I've actually said it out loud and it immediately makes me start to cry. Mom scoots her chair back and comes over to me. She sits down in Jentry's vacant chair and reaches over to pull me toward her. I rest my head on her chest, wishing I could stay here forever.

• • •

Three days later I'm packing my stuff as slowly as humanly possible. I don't want to go back to school. I want to stay here, in my room filled with science fair and spelling bee trophies. I don't want to face the Alphas, or tell Charlie that I know he lied to me. I just want to bury myself under my comforter and stare at my glow-in-the-dark constellations on my ceiling.

"You have to go back. You can either do it with underwear or without," Jentry teases, shoving stuff in my bag.

"I don't belong there," I tell her, feeling sorry for myself.

"You still have me, you know?" she says, making me feel guilty.

"I'm sorry, Jentry. I'm just so scared about how things are going to turn out."

"Everything is going to be fine. Besides, you thought up that awesome science lab thingy, right?"

My science fair idea. Jentry is right; that's something to be excited about. I have until midnight tonight to turn in my application. The science department is open until midnight just for last-minute applicants. Most of the people entering go stand in line instead of mailing their applications. It's kind of a status symbol to get your entry stamped. Last year I had to mail my entry since I was still living at home with my parents, so I'm super psyched that I get to stand in line this year. Who knows, maybe I'll get recognized as last year's winner by a few people. And then I have finals to look forward to in a few weeks.

Most people would cringe at the thought of all-night study sessions, but not me. I've missed immersing myself in my studies. And while my books and good grades will never take the place of the Alphas, at least it's something.

"You girls getting all packed?" Mom asks, peeking her head in my room. Surprisingly, she doesn't seem completely despondent over the idea of me leaving. She even agreed to let us take the bus back to campus.

"I'm going to go say goodbye to Sean," Jentry says, winking at me. Mom hugs her as she passes by, then plops herself down on my bed.

"She's a good friend," Mom says.

"The best," I agree.

"I'm sorry that I didn't always trust you to make your own decisions, Grace Kelly. I should have had more faith in you," Mom says, lowering her head.

"I'm sorry that I didn't listen to you more. I could have saved myself a heck of a lot of heartache," I confess, thinking about my decision to get involved with the Alphas.

"I don't think you should regret any of the decisions you've made. I never could have navigated college when I was your age. I'm really proud of you," she beams.

"You know what? I'm pretty proud of me too," I laugh. She scoops me up in a warm, vanilla-scented hug that I could stay in forever. How could I have hated these hugs so much just a few months ago? Of all the things I expected to learn at college, how much my mom and family mean to me wasn't one of them. But it is definitely a lesson I won't forget.

FOURTEEN

I'm so glad that Jentry thought to pack me this thermos of hot chocolate. I think some of my mom might have rubbed off on her over break. I sip the warm, chocolaty liquid and it takes the edge off how bitterly cold I am.

I'm bundled up in three coats and a blanket, on the sidewalk in front of the science building. I'm fairly certain that I've already entered the first stage of hypothermia but I'm first in line, so I don't really give a crap. It is eleven thirty-seven and the doors open at eleven fifty-five. If your entry isn't stamped by midnight, you're out. Okay, they've never actually turned anyone away yet, but it's still the status thing.

There are thirty-eight people behind me, eyeballing me, just waiting for me to wimp out. So much for any fame or glory here. It's totally cutthroat. But considering tuition money is on the line, that's pretty understandable.

"I wish I could say that I was surprised," I hear a voice say from behind me. I turn to see Charlie grinning mischievously. I hate that I get partial feeling back in my feet from the heat Charlie causes to course through my body. Hormones are such traitors.

"I'm just waiting to kick your butt again," I smart off, promptly turning away from him.

"I like a girl who is confident," he laughs, lowering himself down in front of me.

"Hey, no budging," the guy behind me says. He lowers his Sudoku puzzle book while giving Charlie a warning with his eyes.

"Dude, chill out. I'm just talking to my girlfriend," Charlie defends himself, holding his hands out like he's innocent.

Girlfriend? Did I hear him right or is it so cold that my hearing is now in jeopardy?

"How was your Thanksgiving?" Charlie asks innocently.

I hate that I want to tell him all about my weekend and ask about his. How can he look so adorable in his Carhartt overalls and earmuffs? It isn't fair.

"Do you think I'm stupid?" I ask him, tightening my stocking cap over my ears.

"Um, no," he answers, looking confused.

"So why would you flat out lie to me?" Disgusted, I toss the remaining cocoa in my cup in the grass and screw it back on the container.

"Grace Kelly, I honestly have no idea what you're talking

about." He looks so innocent that I have to resist the urge to kick him.

"When were you going to tell me that you already have a girlfriend? I mean, we're in the same sorority house. Okay, *were* in the same sorority house. Did you really think I wouldn't find out?" My voice is getting louder and I don't seem to be able to control it. Charlie and I are attracting the stares of my fellow science fair participants.

"Are you accusing me of dating someone else?"

"Stop playing dim. I know all about you and Sloane Masterson." I can almost taste bile in my mouth just saying her name.

"Oh, this again?" he groans. "I told you. Sloane and I were only planning the Jingle Bell Run together. I don't know what she thought was going on, but nothing was," he says defensively.

"That's funny, because the Alphas aren't doing the Jingle Bell Run this year." I think I have him with my revelation but as soon as I see the look on his face, I realize that I have been completely wrong. It all makes sense now.

"Sloane is a Zeta, not an Alpha," we both say in unison.

A million memories come flying at me all at once. The fire that would shoot from Sloane's eyes every time an Alpha dissed a Zeta, the Zetas running for Sloane's car when Jentry and I were driving it, her absence at some of our functions. She is trying to infiltrate the Alphas for the Zetas. Once she goes active, she'll know all the Alpha secrets to use against them. I've got to help my sisters.

"I'm really sorry, Charlie. I had it all wrong. I've got

to go fix this," I say, tearing the blanket off and tossing it aside. I stuff the thermos into my old backpack and throw it across my shoulders.

"You can't leave right now. You won't be back in time to enter the science fair."

"This is more important," I tell him, tearing off across campus.

• • •

I realize about halfway across campus that I have absolutely no proof that Sloane is a Zeta. I can't just go barging into the Alpha house with some story. They'll never trust me after what I did. I have to get proof.

The Zeta Sigma Alpha house is a stately, three-story brick Colonial adorned in multicolored twinkle lights. The smoke coming from the chimney immediately dashes my hopes that maybe none of the girls have returned from Thanksgiving break. I sneak around the back of the house to a partially filled parking lot. Three of the ten windows in the back of the house are illuminated. Somehow I have to figure out how I can get proof that Sloane is a Zeta without being noticed by any of the other Zetas. I'm sure they probably have a "Wanted" poster of me hanging in the house after Sloane told them I was the one who sliced their panties. If they bust me, I'm dead.

The back door enters into the kitchen, which looks empty. I get an idea that just might work. I peel off my excess coats and backpack and stash them under the wooden steps leading to the back door. I wrap my hair into a short ponytail and secure it with a rubber band. Quietly I turn the knob to the back door, which luckily pops right open. I tiptoe into the kitchen, leaving the door cracked behind me. I have a feeling I might need a fast exit.

I listen to the sounds of the house but all I hear is the normal creaking, the furnace kicking on, and some faint sounds of music wafting down from the registers. I head for the refrigerator to find something to use to cover my face. That way if a nosy Zeta busts me, she'll just think I'm a fellow sister exfoliating her dead skin. I reach for a tub of guacamole when I hear the stairs in the foyer creaking. I flip the lid off and slather smushed avocado all over my face, leaving small eye and mouth holes.

I hear the kitchen door swing open and I quickly shove the container back on the shelf and bury my face in the fridge. My heart is beating so fast that I'm pretty sure it's visible through my T-shirt. If I make it through this, this is definitely my last undercover task. I guess this is kind of like my last Alpha task, even though technically I'm not an Alpha, nor will I ever be.

"Hand me a water, Katie," a sleepy voice says from behind me. I grab a bottle of water and hand it behind me without turning around. "Thanks," I hear the girl say as she shuffles over to a cabinet. I pretend to investigate my options in the fridge while she rummages through the cabinet.

"Night," she says, shuffling back out of the room. I shut the refrigerator door and take a minute to catch my breath. That was way too close. I have to get my proof on Sloane and get the heck out of here.

I crack the door open and peek out. I don't see anyone so I slip out of the kitchen and head toward the living room. I just need something that puts Sloane in the Zeta house. Some sort of documentation or something. I slide along the hallway wall until I reach the great room.

The Zetas' great room actually looks similar to ours. A plush sectional sits in an L-shape, taking up most of the room. One wall is made up of bookcases filled with framed photos. A plasma television hangs above the still smoldering fireplace. I'm about to investigate other parts of the house when my eyes fall on an eight-by-ten photograph of Sloane wearing a black dress and pearls. Just below the dip of her pearls is a shiny gold Zeta pin. I rush to the bookcase and grab the frame. I skitter back down the hall to the kitchen with my face tightening from the hardening guacamole. I wish I could take the time to wipe my face, but I don't want to spend another second in this house.

I slip quietly out the back door, the frame safely tucked in my arms. I'm practically ecstatic imagining how I'll save the Alphas from leaking their secrets to a mole. Surely they won't be able to hate me after this. I grab my coats and backpack from under the steps. I lay the picture down carefully while I slip into one of the coats because it's freezing. It is bad enough that I have guacamole freezing to my face.

"What do you think you are doing?" a familiar voice says, causing bolts of fear to run through my body.

I turn slowly to see Sloane glaring at me, then glancing to her picture. Confusion registers on her face. Clearly I must really resemble this Katie person, because it takes almost a full second for Sloane to see past the guacamole and recognize my eyes. It gives me just enough time to grab the picture and bolt from the Zeta house.

"I'm going to kill you when I catch up with you," Sloane screams, from not too far behind me. Somehow I don't think she's just saying that.

My mind automatically wants to start figuring out how far the Alpha house is, and at my current rate of speed, how long it will take me to get there. But I shut it down and focus on the physical act of getting to the Alpha house. If I trip, I'm dead. I jump a shrub on the Zeta property line and head toward the front of the house, where I have a better chance of running into more people.

I hear Sloane's shoes crunching the gravel behind mine, then nothing, meaning she jumped the shrub too and is practically close enough to touch me.

"Help me," I start screaming, hoping I'll scare her off.

"Nobody is going to help you," she yells, lunging on my back and knocking me to the ground. I land on top of my arms, which are still holding the picture frame. The weight cracks the glass on the frame. I clutch it tight as Sloane tries to pry my arms from under me.

"It's over, Sloane. I'm telling the Alphas everything," I yell, muffled from having my face kissing the ground.

"You won't be telling anyone anything when I get done with you." She punches me in the side and even though my coat is puffy, it smarts. The punches keep coming until I'm about to give up. Maybe the Alphas won't need proof. Maybe they'll just take my word for it. Yeah, right. I can't believe I failed the Alphas again, but my arms are loosening and I can't hang on anymore.

Just as I'm about to give up the last shred of hold I have on the picture, I can breathe again. Sloane isn't on top of me anymore and the punches have stopped. I struggle to my feet to see Charlie holding Sloane by the collar of her jacket as she tries to connect her left fist to my face. Charlie jerks her back just in time.

"I thought you might need some help," Charlie says, cracking up when he sees my face.

"You're the best boyfriend ever. I gotta go," I yell, taking off toward the Alpha house.

· · ·

I arrive at the Alpha house huffing and puffing, so I take a minute to collect myself before ringing the doorbell. I swipe at my face with my jacket sleeve, but the guacamole is all crusty now so it won't come off. I stab the doorbell quickly, knowing that my nervousness about facing the Alphas is only going to get worse the longer I stand out here. I hear footsteps in the hall and blow out the breath I was holding.

Lindsay swings the door open and eyes me with suspicion. "Grace Kelly?"

"*T* is for traitor," I say, thrusting the picture at her. I ditched the broken frame in a trash can on the way over.

Her eyes scan the picture and when she sees the Zeta pin, she covers her mouth with her hand.

"Why did you—" she begins, then stops.

"Because you're still my sisters," I tell her, walking away.

• • •

Christmas break is finally here. I shove another pair of jeans into my already loaded-down suitcase. I completely aced my finals. I missed the deadline to enter the science fair, but I figure it's time to give someone else a chance anyway. Besides, it gives me my entire break to help Mom decorate, bake, and shop, and also to go out on the occasional date with Charlie.

"So Lindsay is pretty sure that the Zetas are going to get their charter pulled," Jentry beams.

The whole Sloane debacle caused quite a ruckus on campus, even landing her on the front page of the school newspaper. Rumor has it that the Zetas were so furious about her screwing up that they banned her from the house. A few days later, some moving men showed up and cleaned out her dorm room. I wish I could say that I'll miss her next semester, but that would make me a big fat liar.

"I'm pretty sure they would have killed me and buried my body had they caught me inside the house," I say, shivering.

"Yeah, but the Alphas are forever in your debt," Jentry says, zipping her own suitcase. I nod in agreement, trying to ignore the stabbing pain in my chest at the mention of the Alphas.

Lindsay and the other girls sent me a beautiful letter telling me how much they appreciated everything I had done for the house, but I guess I was still expecting to be let back in.

"You look really nice," I tell Jentry, commenting on her black wrap dress and perfectly made-up face and hair. She is spending the holidays with her parents after calling them and airing her feelings. I can tell she's trying to impress them. My eyes linger on the Alpha pin adorning the left side of her dress.

"Aw, this old thing," she laughs, gesturing to the dress. She winks at me, knowing she hasn't fooled me for a second. "So that was super cool of Edwina Fay to send you all that stuff," Jentry says, gesturing to the cardboard box full of the cosmetic company's makeup.

"You're welcome to any of it," I tell her, touching the letter on my desk that was included in the box. Edwina wrote that even though she didn't approve of the way I became an Alpha, she understood. She thanked me for defending the sorority against Sloane. It was nice to be forgiven by her, especially since Charlie and I are getting so close.

"What a semester, huh?" Jentry says, appearing next to me, struggling with her many bags.

"Yeah, who would have guessed," I laugh, remembering the first time I saw her underneath Aaron's dragon tattoo. So many things have changed since then, besides just my hair and makeup. I realize now that you can learn things from life that you'll never be able to learn from a book.

"Ready?" I ask, sliding on my jacket and grabbing my suitcase. "Charlie is waiting downstairs to take us to the bus station."

"Yeah, I know. I told him that I need to run an errand real quick," she says, shutting and locking our door for the last time this semester.

FIFTEEN

"Charlie, can you make a quick detour to the Alpha house?" Jentry calls from the backseat of Charlie's Jeep.

"Alpha house? I thought you meant you needed to go to Walgreen's or something. I don't think this is a very good idea, Jentry," I say nervously.

"It's okay, GK. The sisters are all gone on break. I just have to check and make sure nobody left a flat iron plugged in or anything." Jentry's explanation sounds pretty weak, but Charlie heads toward the Alpha house anyway.

I'm startled when Charlie pulls onto the curb in front of the house instead of using the back parking lot.

"What's the use of having a Jeep if I can't off-road a little bit?" he laughs, noticing my shock.

I open the door and jump out onto the sidewalk. I pull the seat forward to let Jentry out. She delicately pulls herself from the back of the Jeep, trying not to do damage to her dress or heels. I glance at the Alpha house and it looks like Jentry was right. There isn't a light on in the place. Just being so close to the house still stings. I'm starting to wonder if I'll ever feel differently.

"It's kind of creepy with no lights on. Can you come in with me?" Jentry asks, starting to shut the Jeep door.

"Oh, no," I shake my head. It's bad enough just standing outside. I know the Alphas aren't mad at me anymore but I'm sure they wouldn't be too jazzed about me being inside the house either.

"Charlie will go in with you," I offer, raising my eyebrows to plead with him. He shuts off the Jeep and jumps out.

"Let's all go. Safety in numbers," he says teasingly.

"Come on," Jentry says, grabbing the sleeve of my coat so that I can't run away from her. Charlie gets behind me and places his hand reassuringly on the small of my back. Even through my jacket, his touch has a calming effect on me.

When we get to the front door, I can't help but remember the first time I went through it. I would still rather suffer through the eye patch again if it meant getting to stay an Alpha. Jentry swings the door wide open and I realize it's a good thing she is double-checking the house. I can't believe that Lindsay would leave it unlocked before leaving town.

The three of us step into the darkened foyer, where only a night-light illuminates the house. I don't remember that being there before, but I guess I better get used to not knowing what is going on in the house. Charlie kneads my shoulders with his hands, probably knowing how hard being here is for me.

"Thanks for coming in with me, Grace Kelly," Jentry shouts.

"Um, sure. No problem," I respond in a normal voice. She's been acting sort of jittery all night. I think the stress of seeing her parents is finally getting to her.

My stomach plunges when I see the first flicker of light coming from the direction of the great room. But when the melodic chanting of the Alpha song begins, I understand. The Alphas have tricked Jentry into thinking they were gone when really they were waiting here for her initiation ceremony. The original ceremony got canceled after the mess I made of everything. I shouldn't be here. This is a sacred time between sisters.

I know I should bolt out of the house, but my feet seem cemented to the marble floor as one by one the sisters make a circle around the foyer. They're all smiling as they sing about lifelong bonds. When the circle is complete, Lindsay steps forward. She is smiling, so I guess she isn't too upset about me busting in on their party.

When she extends her arm, I think she is going to hand Jentry the unlit candle she's holding. Then I notice that Jentry already has a lit candle in her hands. She's beaming up at me. I'm still not getting what is happening until Lindsay stops directly in front of me and hands me the candle. I look back to Jentry, as if to question whether this is actually happening. She nods her head vigorously.

"Grace Kelly Cook, you have proven to be an extremely loyal pledge. The Alphas would like to extend a lifelong invitation of sisterhood to you. Will you accept?" Lindsay asks, smiling, making my mouth drop to the floor.

This one's a no-brainer. "Absolutely!" I answer, tipping my candle toward hers to light it. She hands off her candle to Jentry, who is beaming brighter than either of the candles she's holding. My fellow sisters and Charlie cheer as Lindsay sticks my Alpha pin onto my collar. Lindsay doesn't even notice that she has to stick it onto the collar of a sweatshirt because I'm so underdressed. GK would have cringed at the inappropriateness of my outfit. But the Alphas don't care about stuff like that. As I glance around the room at my best friend, my boyfriend, and all my new sisters, I realize that I never needed a hypothesis, or a makeover. I just needed to be myself.

Acknowledgments

Thank you to Andrew Karre for believing in this book enough to buy it. Thank you to my incredible editor, Brian Farrey. I knew from the moment we talked that my book was in the hands of someone who truly believed in it. More thanks goes out to everyone at Flux who helped bring this book to life.

I will never be able to thank my brilliant agent, Jenny Bent, enough. You pushed me to make this book the best it could be and you never gave up on it. You have faith in my work when I don't and I couldn't do it without you.

And most of all, thank you to all the booklovers in the world. You make it possible for me to have my dream job.

Warren Hale

About the Author

Stephanie Hale lives in Illinois with her husband and two sons. She enjoys pizza with extra cheese, crisp paperbacks, shaved ice, and the smell of suntan lotion. She hopes her novels make people laugh out loud at very inopportune moments. At the ripe age of twelve, she dreamed of becoming as prolific as Danielle Steel. She's still working on it.